NEIGHBOURS 3

From the car, Helen Daniels stared across the grass at the tall, distinguished-looking man who had just kissed a woman beside the fountain, and sighed. Yes, that was him; that was Douglas Blake. There was no mistake.

She had watched him as he waited by the fountain, glancing every now and again at his wristwatch, then, as the well-dressed woman had walked towards him through the park, he had walked along the path to meet her. He had kissed her in a way that suggested more than mere familiarity.

'Helen, he looks very respectable,' Madge Mitchell observed in a tone of disbelief.

'I thought so too,' Helen said quietly. 'Once.'

Also by Carl Ruhen and available in Star Books

SONS AND DAUGHTERS 1
SONS AND DAUGHTERS 2
SONS AND DAUGHTERS 3
SONS AND DAUGHTERS 4
SONS AND DAUGHTERS 5
SONS AND DAUGHTERS 6
SONS AND DAUGHTERS 7

NEIGHBOURS 1
NEIGHBOURS 2

YOUNG DOCTORS 1

NEIGHBOURS 3

Carl Ruhen

From an original concept by Reg Watson and based on the scripts of Kay Bendle, Helen Carmichael, Peter Connah, Penny Fraser, Ray Harding, Jill James, Ray Kolle, Harold Lander, John Linton, Ginny Lowndes, Greg Millin, Roger Moulton, Christine McCourt, David O'Brien, David Phillips, Philip Ryall, Christine Schofield, Greg Stevens, John Upton, Adrian van den Bok, Reg Watson, Sally Webb.

A STAR BOOK
published by
the Paperback Division of
W.H. ALLEN & Co Plc

A Star Book
Published in 1988
by the Paperback Division of
W.H. Allen & Co Plc
44 Hill Street, London W1X 8LB

Copyright © Horwitz Grahame Pty Ltd, 1988

Printed and bound in Great Britain by
Anchor Brendon Ltd, Tiptree, Essex

ISBN 0 352 32201 2

One

It was bad enough that Madge had turned up out of the blue like that, but then, when the gorilla decided to move in next door, Max Ramsay was even more appalled. It wasn't only the gorilla, a great hairy beast with a touch of the mange, but the human-sized chickens that came along with it. Between Madge and the gorilla – not to mention the chickens – Max wasn't sure which was worse. He felt it was all part of some dark and terrible plot to get at him.

When Madge had telephoned to say she was flying down from the North Coast, and asked if somebody could pick her up from the airport, Max had naturally assumed she would book into a motel somewhere. He didn't expect he would actually have to come face to face with her while she was in the city, comfortable in the motel of her choice, conducting whatever business it was that had brought her there. Sister or not, they had never hit it off together. He had quite happily allowed Shane to pick her up in that fancy company limousine of his and deliver her to wherever she wanted to go. How was he to know then that the place she wanted to go was the place *he* didn't want her to go, namely right here, to his very own house? But there she was, in his kitchen, as large as life, while Shane, to give him his due, was looking quite uncomfortable in his chauffeur's uniform. Max glared at his son. He was already in a foul mood after an hour's wrestling with the lawn mower motor in the back yard.

1

'I thought I told you...'

'After all these years, Max,' Madge broke in calmly, 'I think you could at least be civil.'

Civil? They had been at each other's throats all their lives. 'You didn't say anything about coming *here*!' he replied, advancing threateningly on his son, the chauffeur whose sense of direction left very much to be desired. 'Why did you bring her here?'

'It's not Shane's fault,' Madge said. 'I told him to bring me here.'

Max was still glowering at Shane. 'Great. Well, now, you can take her right back out of here.'

'Oh, come on, Dad...'

'She only means trouble.' He rounded on his sister. 'What did you come here for, anyway?' he demanded.

She stared evenly back at him. 'Because I'm worried. Because I had to learn from strangers that Maria has left you. At least someone could have written to me.' She smiled tightly. 'Not that it came as any great surprise, mind you. Why you ever thought the marriage would have worked out is quite beyond me.'

She hadn't been in the house five minutes and already she was getting at him. 'It lasted twenty years!' Max retorted.

Madge shook her head. 'It was doomed from the day you proposed to her. So beautiful she was, so innocent. Let's face it, Max, any woman would have to be a saint to put up with you.'

Max only just managed to restrain himself from letting her have one right there, fair and square across the chops with the back of his hand. He clenched his fists. His face was heated. Shane said, 'Would you like a cup of tea, Auntie Madge?'

'Like hell she will,' Max growled.

'Thank you, Shane,' Madge said pleasantly. 'Milk, no sugar.'

2

Shane went off to make the tea. 'Anyway, what happened betweeen Maria and me,' Max said, 'is none of your business.'

'Oh, isn't it?' Madge retorted, patches of colour appearing on her cheeks. 'The things that have been going on in this street. You're getting a divorce, and then there was that scandal about a month ago when Paul Robinson was shot by his wife.'

'I still say it's none of your business.'

'You're forgetting that Ramsay Street was named after my grandfather.'

'He was my grandfather, too.'

Madge was clearly angry now. They faced each other across the kitchen table. 'Yes, and look what you've let this street be reduced to,' she accused him. 'Murder, divorces, and God knows what else. He'll be turning in his grave.'

'Which won't be easy, seeing you cremated him.'

Shane had made the tea. He placed a cup on the table in front of Madge. 'Dad, I've got to get back to work,' he said.

'Good. Then you can drop her off somewhere.'

Madge turned to Shane. 'Perhaps you could bring my luggage in before you go.'

'Oh no you won't,' Max shouted. 'There's no way she's staying in this house.' He looked at Madge and emphasised this by pointing dramatically to the door.

Madge remained unmoved. 'Rant and rave all you like, Max,' she said equably. 'I'm staying here.' She nodded to Shane. 'He'll be all right.'

Shane was looking inquiringly at his father. 'Well, Dad?'

'Take her to a motel,' Max commanded furiously.

Madge was still unshaken. 'Bring in the luggage, Shane,' she ordered, then turned back to her brother. 'I think you've forgotten something, Max,' she said quietly

3

but firmly. 'I know where the body's buried.'

It was more than a jab; it was a body blow. He hadn't seen her for five years, and now here she was, in his own house, calmly preparing to move in and telling him she knew where the body was buried. He felt just about ready to explode. But through his fury a small voice was telling him that it was no time to talk about buried bodies, not in front of Shane, or anyone else. He would give her twenty-four hours, no more. He stormed out through the back door to give vent to his rage on the recalcitrant lawn mower.

There were people moving into the house next door. When he saw the removal van pull up outside, Max was curious. He sauntered across to it, to where two men were just lowering the tail gate. 'Good day.'

'Good day.' The older of the two men put away the list he had been consulting and took a set of keys from his pocket. He began to walk towards the house. Max followed him hopefully.

'Someone moving in, are they?'

The removal man sighed and stopped walking. 'Live around here, do you?'

'Right next door,' Max replied. 'I was just wondering what the new neighbours are like.'

The removal man regarded him knowingly for a moment, then shook his head. 'Sorry. In this job, we see all and say nothing. Our lips are sealed. Professional ethics, the spirit of confidentiality – that's why people trust us. But whenever we deliver furniture, there's always one joker who wanders up and wants to know what the new people are like, what the furniture's like, have they got a dog – that one's usually high on the list.'

Max didn't like dogs. He'd had trouble with dogs before, so he wasn't altogether surprised by the revelation. 'I hope for their sake they *don't* have a dog,' he remarked gruffly.

4

'I've got three dogs myself,' the removal man said casually. 'I *like* dogs.'

Realising he wasn't going to get any more information from this source, Max turned away. 'Then you're lucky, mate, that *you're* not trying to move into the street,' he offered as a parting shot. He was out of sorts; it clearly wasn't his day. His only consolation was the fact that Madge had only another eighteen hours and forty-five minutes before her time was up. Another eighteen hours and forty-five minutes, and out she would be, bag and baggage, on her way back home, sorrier but wiser. Max rubbed his hands together. That was something, anyway.

Later that afternoon, he was working on the engine of his van in the driveway at the front of his house, while at the same time keeping an eye open for any sign of movement from the house next door in front of which now stood a small and battered Honda Civic garishly painted over with stripes and flowers that were reminiscent of another age.

'Hello, Max.'

Lifting his head out from beneath the raised bonnet of his van, Max straightened and nodded to Helen Daniels who, carrying a shopping bag, had stopped at the end of the drive. 'Helen,' he said.

Helen nodded towards the car of many colours. 'I see the new neighbours have arrived.'

Max was wiping his grease-stained hands with an old rag. 'Yeah. I haven't seen them yet. That eyesore was there when I came out to fix...' he jerked his head towards the exposed engine of his van ... 'this.'

'I hear Madge is staying with you,' Helen Daniels said.

'Bad news travels fast,' Max returned grimly.

'Don't tell me you two are *still* arguing.'

'Arguing?' Max tossed the rag into the cabin of the

van. 'We've been at daggers drawn ever since we clapped eyes on each other nearly forty years ago.' He shook his head in exasperation. 'I tell you, Helen, that woman may be a moral crusader, but she'd drive any man to drink after ten minutes.'

Behind him, the front door opened and he heard quick footsteps on the path. 'Helen!' Madge called. 'Hello! How nice to see you again after all these years.'

Wiping her hands on the apron she had put on to do the washing up, she hurried up to them. 'And it's nice to see *you* again, Madge,' Helen said, smiling back at her. 'How long are you staying?'

'What time is it now?' Max asked sarcastically. The hours were dragging by far too slowly.

'Don't take any notice of him,' Madge said, giving her brother a hard look. 'I'm staying long enough to help Max and the boys get back on their feet again.'

'Get on our *feet*?' Max cried angrily. There she was, at it again, rubbing him up the wrong way. 'What the hell is *that* supposed to mean?'

Helen was beginning to look a little uneasy. Madge said, 'Well, no man finds it easy to settle down after his wife has walked out on him.'

Bloody cheek! Bloody hide! 'This has nothing to do with you, Madge,' Max snapped. 'I just wish you'd clear off back to those wowser friends of yours and leave Ramsay Street alone.'

Ignoring him, Madge addressed Helen Daniels. 'And Ramsay Street certainly isn't what it used to be – is it, Helen?'

'Oh, I don't know ...'

Just then there was a sharp report from a backfiring engine, and the three of them turned just in time to see the hideously painted little car that had been standing outside the house next door driving off down the street. 'There,' Max cried out in annoyance. 'Now look at what

6

you've gone and done. I've got neighbours I haven't even clapped eyes on because of you.' Slamming down the hood of his van he turned and stomped angrily up the path to the front door of the house. It was definitely not his day at all.

He was still fuming when, about ten minutes later, Madge made tea for them both. 'I brought a surprise for you,' she said as Max emerged from the bathroom after washing his hands. She nodded to a plate of homemade biscuits on the kitchen table. 'They used to be your favourites when you were a little boy – remember?'

Max didn't want to remember. She wasn't going to get around him as easily as that. 'I don't like biscuits.'

'Of course you do. They're our mum's recipe.'

'The old man broke his teeth on her biscuits.'

Madge decided it was time to appeal to reason. 'Max,' she said, not unkindly, 'why don't we both make the most of this situation?' Max said nothing and sipped his tea. Madge went on, 'I really thought I would be able to comfort you and the boys when I heard that Maria had walked out on you.'

'She didn't walk out,' Max retorted. 'She drove off in a taxi – with my blessing.'

Madge smiled at him across the table. 'Yes, she would have your blessing. That's one thing about you, Max; you really loved Maria – and I can understand how your pride won't let you admit how hurt you are by what happened.'

'Why don't you go home?'

'It hasn't been a good year for you, has it?' Madge continued. 'Shane's accident... I remember Maria telling me how obsessed you were about him becoming an Olympic diving champion. And now look at him. A chauffeur.'

'There's nothing wrong with him being a chauffeur,'

7

Max was stung to reply. 'And there's nothing wrong with me being a plumber.' He glared at her. 'And anyway, for all your airs and graces, look at what *you* married – a traffic warden, for heaven's sake.'

'You're impossible, Max,' Madge said with a sigh. 'I'm your only sister, and I want to help you – but we just can't communicate, can we?'

Pushing back his chair, Max stood up. 'Okay, so you want to communicate,' he said harshly. 'I'll tell you what I'll do then. You go back and take care of your family, and I'll write you a long letter. If I can only just get you out of my hair, I'll communicate like mad – by post.'

Leaving her with the tea and the untouched plate of home-made biscuits, Max left the house and walked down the driveway to the footpath where, earlier, his younger son, Danny, had left a wheelbarrow filled with weeds he had pulled out of the garden. As he was about to trundle the wheelbarrow to the rear of the house, he noticed that the multi-coloured car was once again parked outside the house next door. He was puzzled. Whoever the new people were, they were certainly being very elusive.

Danny was weeding the back garden. As Max tipped the contents of the wheelbarrow onto a pile near the fence, he looked up. 'I'll do all that, Dad. You don't have to help me.'

'I'll do anything to keep out of that woman's way,' Max stated emphatically.

Danny pulled out another handful of weeds. 'Auntie Madge is very strait-laced, isn't she?' he observed.

'Proper battle-axe she is,' Max said with feeling. 'I feel sorry for the poor mug who married her.'

'I don't remember him.'

'No, she always left him up at Coffs Harbour – looking after the kids. She...' He stopped; he had just heard a very unusual sound. 'Hey, what's that?'

8

'What's what?'

'Listen.' He stared at the fence that separated his property from next door.

And there it was again – a deep growling sound that came from the other side of the fence. Max was mystified; he hadn't heard anything like it before. But whatever it was, it didn't sound at all friendly. He looked at Danny. Danny looked back at him. There was another rumble from behind the fence. Max hurried across to the fence, and kneeling on the ground, peered through a crack between the wooden slats. He started, his eyes wide in amazement.

What he found himself staring at were two very large and very hairy feet that certainly didn't belong to any human. He saw very long, crooked toenails that were quite black. 'Hey, Danny,' he whispered urgently, beckoning to his son without taking his eye from the crack in the fence. 'Take a look at this.'

As Danny came to his side, Max straightened and pointed to the hole in the fence. Danny knelt where his father had knelt and peered through the hole while Max waited for his reaction. 'What am I supposed to be looking at?' he asked after a brief pause.

'The hairy legs.'

'Hairy legs?' Danny chuckled. 'What hairy legs?'

Pushing him to one side, Max knelt once more in front of the hole. The hairy legs had gone. He looked at Danny who was watching him with an expression of uncertain amusement. 'Come on, Dad, what's the joke?'

'Two hairy legs,' Max said impatiently. 'That's what I saw. It looked like a . . .'

'A spider?'

Max straightened. 'Of course it wasn't a spider, you clown,' he snarled. He turned away and began to head determinedly towards the front of the house. 'I'm going in to see these new neighbours. This mystery is about to

9

be solved.'

'Hang on, Dad,' Danny called after him. 'I'll come with you.'

But the mystery wasn't about to be solved – not right then, anyway. Max knocked on the front door of the house next door, and rang the bell, but there was no response. He kept knocking and ringing the bell, but there was still no sign of life from inside the house. It was all very strange.

'The car's there, so they've *got* to be inside,' he said with a puzzled shake of his head. 'There's something weird about these people,' he muttered, 'and I'm going to find out what it is.' He moved along the porch to the front window. He tried to peer in through it, but the curtains were drawn.

'Dad!'

Max straightened a little guiltily. 'Yeah, well, the least people can do when their neighbours pay a call on them is to answer the door.' He gestured dismissively and moved back down the porch. 'Ah, to hell with them.'

Early the following morning, Max was working once more under the hood of his van when he noticed two rather attractive young women walking up the front path of the house next door. Wondering if they were the new neighbours, he watched them as they climbed the steps to the front door. Something very peculiar was going on in there, he decided again. One would think that new neighbours, hairy legs or not, would at least make themselves known to the other people in the street. It was traditional, it was the *courteous* thing to do. Sourly, he returned to adjusting his fan belt. But if that was the way they wanted to behave, then it was no skin off his nose.

He had just slammed down the hood and was about to go back into the house for his breakfast when he was attracted by a movement from the house next door. He stopped and looked. He stared. *Now*, for God's sake, what was happening?

And so it was that Max Ramsay, his heart thumping and the blood rushing to his head, first set startled eyes on the gorilla that had moved in next door – the same gorilla which, with its head tucked under its arm, and in the company of two outsized chickens, was now making its way towards the car that had been painted over in many colours. He gaped at the bulky, furry body as it lumbered down the path, the chickens, all feathers and beak, following close behind. He was stunned at the sight of this mobile menagerie in Ramsay Street in the early morning. Then, as he continued to stare at this bizarre spectacle, he realised that out of the thick – and in places patchy – fur on the body of this creature from the jungle there emerged a rather tousled human head.

The chickens were climbing into the car. Max rushed forward as the gorilla was moving around to the driver's side. 'Hey, you!' he shouted. 'Just hold it right there for a minute.'

The gorilla looked at him curiously – or rather, the human face that crowned this furry phenomenon watched him with partly raised eyebrows. 'Good morning,' the creature greeted him politely. 'You must be my new neighbour.'

'I'm Max Ramsay.'

The human face grinned pleasantly. 'Hi, Max. I'm Clive Gibbons.' A hairy paw was extended towards Max who regarded it with distrust.

'Gibbons? Gorilla?' Max didn't know what to think.

The gorilla gave him a wry smile. 'It's all been said before.'

Inside the car, the chickens were watching Max with interest. Max was still staring at the gorilla. 'What are you?' he demanded angrily. 'Some kind of a nut?'

His new neighbour winked at him. 'Early morning booking, Max.'

'Booking for what?'

'Gorilla telegrams. And chicken ones.' He smiled reassuringly at the poultry inside the car. 'You name it, we do it. We've got to get to the airport now to frighten the hell out of some soccer star.'

Max was thunderstruck. 'You mean, you're running a business from that house?'

'That's right.' Clive nodded. 'Just as I understand that you're running a plumbing business from *your* house.'

So he had already learnt something about Max, who now felt at a disadvantage. He wondered who had provided the newcomer with this piece of information. 'That's different. This street was named after my grandfather.'

'It was?' Clive looked impressed. 'Gee, Max,' he said in a tone of wonderment, 'you're a celebrity.' He opened the car door. 'We'll have to get together some time and talk about it.' He smiled again as he eased his furry bulk into the small car which already seemed to be full of feathers. 'You know, I thought you were deliberately avoiding me.'

Still stunned, hardly believing what had happened, Max stood on the road and stared at the car as it drove away down the street towards the airport and the unsuspecting soccer star. Down his street. This street, which had been named after his grandfather who, by now, with the arrival of this transplanted zoo, must really be turning over in his grave. Then Max remembered again that his grandfather had been cremated, not that that made it any better, of course.

For the rest of that day, Max fumed. He complained and muttered dire threats. He christened the house next door the Ape House, which he thought was very apt. He was waiting outside when the garish little car with its cargo of fur and feathers returned to the Ape House that afternoon. He watched as the two chickens hurried into the house while the gorilla retrieved its head from the back seat, then, in a manner that suggested it was out of sorts about something, slammed the door shut.

Max intercepted him between the car and the footpath. 'Mr Gibbons.'

With its head once more under its arm, the gorilla lacked its former bounce. In fact, it seemed quite depressed. 'Oh, hi, Max,' it said in a voice that lacked expression.

His hands on his hips, Max faced him squarely. 'I'd just like to give you a neighbourly word of advice.'

'Great,' Clive said unenthusiastically. 'Look, could we have a drink some time later?' He glanced up at the house where no doubt the chickens were shedding their feathers. 'I've got to pay off the girls.'

'It's *about* the girls,' Max told him sternly. 'And you.'

'What about us?' A wary look appeared in Clive Gibbons' quite unremarkable eyes.

'Some of the neighbours don't like the way you're turning this street into a zoo.'

Clive shrugged. The wary look vanished. 'Oh, sorry about that. Who are they? I'll go and tell them to mind their own bloody business.'

Max hedged. Though he hadn't spoken to the neighbours, he nevertheless regarded himself as their spokesman; he was very proprietorial about his street. His finger, he felt, was quite firmly on the pulse. 'They wouldn't like that, either,' he replied.

'I see.' Clive regarded him shrewdly. 'You're their spokesman, are you?'

'Yes, I suppose I am.' Max thoughtfully scratched his jaw. 'Yes.'

'Good.' Now there was a hardness in Clive's eyes, a tension in his voice. 'Well, look, Max, I've just been out

13

to the airport on a wild goose chase.' Max flinched; God's creatures were not only being flung at him literally but figuratively as well. Clive went on undeterred. 'The guy the chickengram was for didn't show, and we didn't get paid.' He nodded towards the house. 'I have to pay those two girls out of my own pocket or they won't work for me again.' He fixed Max with a steely stare. 'And the last straw is for a bunch of busybodies to start whingeing about their street looking like a zoo.'

'This street was named after my grandfather,' Max declared, gesturing expansively at the street in question.

Clive sighed wearily. 'That's the second time you've told me that today,' he said in a tone of mild reproach. 'Listen, Max, I had to leave my last place because of a guy just like you, so I understand what you're about.' His voice was rising. 'You don't care *what* people do as long as they do it your way.' He shook his head. 'You'll find I'm a good neighbour, Max, as long as you leave me alone. But if you butt into my life, all hell will be let loose in this street.' He patted Max paternally on the shoulder, then turned away. 'Have a nice day.'

Max stared after him as he walked into the house, not quite sure what he was supposed to make of all that.

Sunday morning was Max's only chance to lie in. He looked forward to his Sunday mornings, lying in bed and knowing he didn't have to get up for anything except, eventually, a late breakfast. He could lounge about in his pyjamas and not bother to shave. Sunday mornings were very special to Max. But this particularly Sunday morning was anything but special.

It was the noise that awoke him – a banging, a thumping, loud music, a piano and drums over which someone was yelling at full voice, 'Right, one and two and one and two and left that claw, flap that wing, that's right, one and two and . . .' Max swore, and flinging back

14

the blankets, sprang out of bed, his Sunday morning in a complete shambles.

'Danny,' he shouted furiously as he wrenched open his bedroom door. 'Turn that damned radio down.'

'It's not me,' Danny called back from the kitchen.

Max stormed into the kitchen where Danny was sitting at the table, brooding about something. 'Right, that's it,' he exclaimed, heading for the radio. 'The only chance I get for a lie-in, and I cop that racket.' Reaching the radio, he pushed the button. But to his astonishment, his ears were blasted by a fresh onslaught of music. He pushed the button again, and the music stopped. But the original racket was still going on. He looked at the radio – and then it finally hit him that the din was coming from next door. He crossed to the window.

'You mongrel,' he yelled. 'Turn that stuff off.'

'I don't think he can hear you, Dad,' Danny said mildly.

'He can hear me all right,' Max snarled, then bellowed through the window again. 'Turn that bloody thing off.'

The noise didn't abate. Max was shaking with rage. He shouted again. Madge came into the room behind him. 'What do you think you're doing?' she demanded.

Max swung on her belligerently. 'What does it look like?'

Madge was quite smartly dressed; she had been out. 'I shudder to think,' she said, distastefully eyeing Max in his pyjamas.

Danny changed the subject. 'Where have you been, Auntie Madge?' he asked.

'To church.'

That would be right, Max thought sourly; that was his sister all over. 'Typical,' he growled. The noise continued to boom into the room from the house next door. Swinging back to the window, Max shook his fist at it. 'That's it,' he cried. 'I've had enough.' He headed for

15

the door.

'Where do you think *you're* going?' Madge was blocking his way.

'To give that gorilla a piece of my mind.'

'I wouldn't be too generous with it, Max,' Madge said drily. 'You don't have so much to give away.'

Max's expression was meant to be withering, but it didn't seem to have any effect. 'Very funny,' he growled, pushing past her and making for the front door.

The closer Max got to the Ape House, the louder the noise became. He could hear the gorilla himself, crying, 'That's it, that's the way. Kick and shake, and one and two and . . .' Max made his own contribution to the ruckus by pounding fiercely on the front door. 'Very good, Joanie, just try to lift your leg a little higher. And one and two and . . .' Max was still banging on the door. The music continued.

He was just about to try kicking the door, when suddenly it opened, and there was Clive Gibbons, looking quite strange without his gorilla costume, glaring out at him. Max launched straight into the attack. 'It's about time you answered,' he shouted.

'It's my door,' Clive returned shortly. 'I'll do what I like with it.'

'Is that right?' Max was itching to get at him. 'Do you know what time it is?'

'It's after eight o'clock.'

'And what's more, it's Sunday.'

'So?'

'So it's my day of rest.'

Clive gave him a crooked smile. 'Some people *are* lucky. I have to work. Now, if you don't mind . . .'

Max pushed forward before Clive had a chance to close the door in his face. 'I not only *mind*, I'm as mad as a cut snake.'

Clive nodded slowly, as if something had just been

16

confirmed to him. 'The neighbours told me about that.'

Max stared at him. 'Who?'

'Nearly everyone I've run into,' Clive replied. 'You've got quite a reputation as a nosy-parker as well.' He jerked his head towards the hallway behind him. 'Do you want to come in and see what I'm doing?'

Max was aghast. His confidence had just taken a terrible dive. He was flustered. He blustered. He said, 'Now listen here; I want you to stop that noise right now.'

'I'm well within the law,' Clive said evenly. 'Which is more than I can say for you, Max.'

'What do you mean?'

'You're trespassing on my property,' Clive pointed out. 'And I'd appreciate your leaving. I'm a busy man.'

Max was fit to be tied. 'I'm not taking this lying down,' he shouted.

'That's what Sundays are for, Max.' Clive was smiling at his neighbour in a most infuriating way. 'Why don't you enjoy it instead of bothering me?'

Then, before Max could think of a suitable retort to that gratuitous piece of advice, the door was closed firmly in his face. He stomped off back across the lawn to his own house, the blaring music providing a mocking accompaniment as he went. The battle lines had been drawn. Total war had been declared.

His mood hadn't much improved by the time he had taken a shower. 'The hide of that bloke, calling me a sticky beak,' he complained bitterly to Madge. 'I've always minded my own business.'

Madge looked up from the book she was reading. 'It'll teach you to go roaming around the neighbourhood in your pyjamas.'

Danny was looking worried about something. Max threw the towel with which he had been drying his hair at him to attract his attention. 'What's wrong with you?

Lovesick, or something?'

Danny nodded glumly. 'More or less.'

Max tried to look understanding. 'I was a bit of a wild lad in my day, too, I can tell you.'

Danny didn't look particularly impressed by this. Madge said, helpfully, 'It was in kindergarten, and all he did was fight – so I wouldn't take too much notice of him, Danny.'

Max gave her another withering look, then sitting down beside Danny, prepared himself for a friendly father and son chat. The music next door had stopped. Max was beginning to feel benign. 'Who is she?'

'A girl at my computer course,' Danny told him.

'Yeah.' Max nodded sagely. 'Those courses are great for that sort of thing, aren't they? I can't tell you the number of women I met when I was at Tech.'

Madge looked up from her book again. 'He used to fix their dripping taps,' she explained to Danny. 'That's why he got such a high mark in his practicals.'

'What would *you* know about it?' Max snapped, the benign feeling slipping away from him.

'We were all proud of you,' Madge said. 'In those days,' she added after a brief but telling pause.

Max decided to ignore her; she was only trying to goad him. He turned back to Danny. 'Go on, son.'

'Well, we were watching that show on television . . . you know, Perfect Match,' Danny said, playing with the salt cellar. 'Marcie said she'd be off like a rocket if someone offered her a chance to go to Surfers' Paradise, so . . .'

Max was way ahead of him. 'Flaming heck!' he exclaimed. Even Madge was looking startled.

'So I was wondering if you would loan me the money to go.'

'He most certainly will not,' Madge said sharply.

Max bridled. What right had *she* to decide what he

could or couldn't do? 'Oh, won't I?'

'The girl sounds just too common,' Madge sniffed.

'Common, eh?' Max was rising to the challenge. 'What would *you* know about it?'

Madge was steadfast in her righteousness. 'No girl worth a pinch of salt would make a suggestion like that to a young man.'

Deciding that here was a way he could get back at Madge, Max pulled out his wallet, from which he extracted a twenty-dollar note. 'I suppose I *could* lend you twenty bucks,' he told Danny.

'Thanks, Dad,' Danny said, pocketing the money. He stood up and left the room, apparently deciding to get out while the going was good and before his father changed his mind.

Madge was watching Max coldly. 'How could you?'

'What's wrong with it?' Max was feeling quite pleased with himself. 'It's only a bit of a trip.'

'You're encouraging wickedness.'

'It's my money,' Max said defensively.

'It's sinful and immoral.'

'You don't mind me keeping you in style with it,' Max said, wilfully misunderstanding her.

'I beg your pardon.'

'So I wouldn't get uppity about it.'

Madge drew herself up; she looked quite formidable. 'I earn my keep, Max,' she said with awesome dignity, 'which is more than I can say for you.'

Max looked at her blankly. 'What are you talking about now?'

'I thought that you, above all, would know that one should neither a borrower nor a lender be.'

Oh, so that was it, a little dig, a gentle reminder that he owed her money. She had to go; Max couldn't take any more of it; he had had enough; he had to turn his mind to ways of getting rid of her. Shane would have to move back into the house for a start; the more people he could get on his side, the better it would be.

Another person whose aid he thought of enlisting for the cause was Helen Daniels next door. Helen was solid; she was a brick; she was a grandmother; Max had always gotten along well with her; she would come up with something. He found her in the kitchen of the Robinson house. Jim Robinson was out at the front of the house, trying to get that hydraulic jack he had invented to work – not apparently, from what Max had seen, with much success.

'You know how I'm a reasonable sort of bloke,' Max told Helen who was drying the lunchtime dishes. 'How I get along well with everyone.' Helen's face was impassive. 'Well, Madge has got me stumped,' Max said.

'Why's that?'

'I don't know.' Max shook his head. 'If I say something is white, she says it's black. She's the most difficult woman I've ever had to deal with.'

Helen's face was still giving nothing away. 'What exactly is the problem?' she asked carefully.

'She's got her nose in everyone else's business for a start.'

'I see.' Helen draped the tea towel over the rack and took off her apron.

'For instance,' Max went on, warming to his theme, 'young Danny's really keen on this girl he met at work.' He chuckled softly. 'Reckons he's going to take her to Surfers' for the weekend. Can you imagine that?'

'Well, he *is* growing up,' Helen remarked tentatively.

'He'll never save up the money,' Max said, 'but does that stop Madge? No, it doesn't. She starts on him about mortal sin, all that sort of thing. Cripes, a bloke can't even have a beer when he gets home from work.'

'Well, what are you going to do about Danny?' Helen asked him.

'I gave him twenty dollars towards the trip. I can't discourage the boy. It's the first time in his life he's ever saved a cent. But it's Madge I'm worried about. I'm a very accommodating sort of fellow, and I know she's my only sister and that...'

'And you'd like to do the right thing by her,' Helen finished for him.

'That's right.' Max nodded, then came to the purpose of his visit. 'I was... ah... wondering if you could find out if she'd like to go back to Coffs Harbour. I'll give her the money for the trip,' he added hastily.

'What if she doesn't want to go?' Helen pointed out.

'You're really good at that sort of thing, Helen,' Max said persuasively.

Helen thought about this for a moment. 'Perhaps I *could* sound her out...'

Max grinned at her. Of course he had known she would come up trumps. 'Gee thanks, Helen. I know you can do it.' He moved towards the door. 'I'm getting Shane to give up that flat of his and move back into the house. That way, there'll be no room for her any more.'

'I see.'

Max opened the door. 'Thanks a lot, Helen. You've no idea how difficult that woman is to deal with.'

Outside, Jim Robinson was still working on his hydraulic jack under the car. He pressed a button; nothing happened. 'You'll never get that thing to work,' Max brightly informed him.

Jim grunted and frowned down at his new invention. 'Well, it's now or never.'

Max watched with interest as Jim vainly tried to make the thing work. 'I don't know why you bother.'

'Nothing ventured, nothing gained,' Jim muttered. 'Look, Max, is there something you want? I'm pretty busy.'

Max became serious. 'I was wondering what you

intend to do about the Ape House.'

'The Ape House?'

'Number twenty-two.'

'They're not doing any harm.'

'Not to you, they're not,' Max said shortly. 'They keep me awake all night, and I want something done about them. And don't tell me to go and tell them to be quiet. I've already done that.'

'Have you tried asking them nicely?' Jim was still fiddling and adjusting.

'That'd be right,' Max said bitterly. 'I knew you'd side with them.'

'I'm doing nothing of the kind.'

'Well, if the neighbourhood won't help me,' Max said loftily, 'I'll have to fix them myself, good and proper.' He wasn't quite sure how he would do this but he would think of something.

He was about to turn away, when suddenly, the hydraulic jack began to lift. Jim beamed in triumph. Then, just as suddenly, the jack dropped again, and Jim's smile vanished. Max felt much better.

If Max thought it would be a simple enough matter to send his sister packing, he had seriously underestimated that good woman. He wasn't about to get rid of her so easily, not after what she had seen. There were things happening in that house that needed straightening out, that needed her firm but guiding hand. The place was going to the dogs, immorality was rife – and all Max seemed to be doing was encouraging it. Madge had a duty to perform; she owed it to the Ramsay family name to do what she could to maintain some form of standards in that household – and if Shane *was* coming back, as Helen Daniels had suggested to her, then he would just have to share Danny's room.

Max had just caught the tail end of a telephone

conversation when he came back into the house later that afternoon – or rather, he had just caught Madge's half of it, and she had sounded quite mysterious. He had heard her say something about visiting hours, and were they the same on a Sunday as they were during the week? Visiting hours for what? Was someone in hospital? When she saw him Madge had quickly replaced the receiver.

'Who was that on the phone?' Max demanded.

'For me to know and for you to find out.'

'It's my flamin' phone,' Max muttered resentfully.

Madge's lips were set in a grim line. 'You'll have to get your own tea tonight,' she said. 'I'm going out and I may be a little late.'

'You can stay away forever for all I care,' Max said with a careless shrug.

She gave him a pitying look. 'And while I'm away, you might like to help Danny put up a spare bed for Shane.'

'Eh?'

She smiled humourlessly. 'I'm awake to your silly little games, Max,' she said. 'I suppose you thought that if Shane moved back, I'd be forced to leave.' Max was stunned. He had already spoken to Shane, who had agreed to come back. It was all set. Madge picked up her bag from the sideboard. 'And we all know why, don't we?' she said meaningfully as she swept out of the room.

There it was again – the implied threat. She thought she had him over a barrel – and the trouble was, she did. Max swore and thumped his fist down on the kitchen table. He winced.

It seemed that everyone had turned against him. Now it was Danny's turn. Max felt betrayed.

Danny knew very well what his father thought of Clive Gibbons who kept such peculiar hours, made so much noise, and went out dressed as a gorilla. 'Don't see why he can't get a decent job like everyone else,' Max had said

23

to Danny in disgust.

'If you'd only talk to him instead of yelling,' Danny had suggested, 'you'd find he's an okay guy.'

Max had eyed him suspiciously. 'Whose side are you on, anyway?'

'There shouldn't be any sides. Why can't you just learn to get on with people?'

That was dangerous talk that could lead to all sorts of pitfalls. 'He's *not* people,' Max had exclaimed in irritation at his son's obtuseness. 'And when we're feuding, I expect you to back me up.'

Which Danny certainly wasn't doing this morning, Max saw now to his dismay as he brought some equipment from the back of the house to load in his van. There they were, chatting away at the front gate of the Ape House, plotting something no doubt. Max scowled at his son – consorting with the enemy! 'Rotten little turncoat,' he muttered to himself as he angrily flung the equipment into the back of the van and stomped back into the house.

That night the Ramsay household was the scene of a very strange occurrence. Max was convinced that a burglar had broken in. It was the sound of something falling in the living room that jolted him awake. Then there was another crash as something topped and shattered. Max's reaction was immediate. Burglars! Launching himself out of the bed, he rushed for the door. 'Shane!' he roared. 'Get up! There's a burglar in the house!' He ran out into the passage, and then into the kitchen where he grabbed a monkey wrench from a shelf before charging on into the living room from where the crashing sounds had come. 'Shane! Danny! Get in here!'

The standard lamp was lying across the floor. A vase had smashed, and flowers were strewn over the carpet. Suddenly, in the dim light that filtered into the room, Max noticed a bulge in one of the full-length window curtains. Aha, he thought as he advanced on the bulge with monkey wrench upraised. 'Yo!' he cried triumphantly as he threw himself at the bulging curtain, 'got you now.'

The struggle was short and unsuccessful. There was a squawk from behind the curtain, a sudden movement – and then, as he grappled with the squirming object, Max suddenly found himself in the thick, smothering material as his weight against the curtain brought it down on top of him. He fought desperately to escape, but succeeded only in entangling himself even more. He bellowed, he roared, and caught a glimpse of a scampering chicken. He struggled some more, and the curtain completely covered him again. He heard footsteps. Someone was reaching for him. He lashed out through the curtain.

'Stop it, Dad!' It was Shane's voice. 'It's me!'

'About time.' Max's voice was muffled by the curtain. 'Did you catch the chicken?'

'Keep still, Max,' Madge said briskly, 'so we can untangle you.'

Max stopped struggling, and a moment later Madge and Shane had him extricated from the curtain. Max tried to sit up. There was a stab of pain in the small of his back. 'I'll sue him, that's what I'll do,' he groaned rubbing his back. 'Grievous bodily harm. Oh, my back.'

Danny came into the room in his pyjamas. 'Sue who? What's all the fuss about?'

Max was clutching something in his other hand. He looked down at the handful of feathers which he must have grabbed in the course of the struggle. 'That chicken farmer next door.' He held up the feathers. 'See?' He struggled to his feet. 'Oh, my back,' he moaned as the effort provoked a more violent twinge. 'First thing in the morning I'm going in there. I've got the evidence.' He brandished the tell-tale feathers again. 'Let's see how he explains *this* away.'

The following morning he was at the house next door bright and early. The sun had barely risen and the dew was still glistening on the grass. He moved slowly across the lawn, getting his bare feet wet and holding his back, which wasn't really so painful now – but the gorilla couldn't be expected to know that. He held the feathers like a bouquet in his other hand.

As soon as the front door of the Ape House opened and Clive Gibbons blinked sleepily out at him, Max thrust the feathers in his face. 'You can't get out of this one,' he snarled. 'I've got the evidence.'

Clive took the feathers from Max and looked at them with a puzzled frown. 'One of the flock been moulting?' he asked. 'Must be getting broody.'

'Getting broody all right,' Max cried. 'In my home. Breaking and entering, it was.' He was still holding his back.

'Must have got the houses mixed up,' Clive suggested calmly. 'I'll put a luminous number on mine – how's that? That should stop any confusion.'

'*Confusion*?' Max shouted. 'It was more than confusion. Knocked over half the furniture.' He turned slightly. 'And look at my back.' Clive looked at his back. 'Nearly broke it, that's what he did. I've got a good mind to call the police.'

'I don't see what they can do,' Clive pointed out. 'Your back looks okay, and you haven't mentioned any broken door or window, so you must have left the house unlocked for any unsuspecting chicken to just walk in.'

It was true that there was no sign of forced entry; Max had checked. But Clive's reasonable approach to the subject only made him more enraged. 'Won't you take *any* responsibility?'

'Of course I'll pay for the damages,' Clive replied. 'I'd hate us to become enemies over this, Mr Ramsay.'

'We already *are* enemies,' Max informed him. 'And if

one of your chickens, or any of your other animals, sets foot in my house again, I'll ... I'll ...'

'You'll send it back?'

'No. I'll call the RSPCA.'

When Madge confided in Max her worries about Danny, he feigned indifference – but he was, in fact, most concerned. Somehow or other, Danny had got hold of a considerable amount of money, two hundred bucks or more. Madge had discovered this quite by accident. She had picked up his wallet from his bedroom floor where it had fallen, and it had accidentally opened. Quite a lot of money, she said. Naturally, she didn't mean to pry, but she couldn't help but notice.

'So he's been saving.' Max covered his surprise with a shrug.

'That's nonsense, and you know it,' Madge said crisply. 'It was only a couple of days ago that he was complaining about not having any money.'

That was right; when he wanted to take some chick north to Surfers' Paradise for a doubtful weekend, Max had given him twenty bucks. He regarded his sister coolly. 'What are you saying, Madge? That he stole it?'

'Of course not,' Madge said quickly. 'Although, heaven knows, the unsavoury company he's been keeping lately might lead him to do anything.'

Angrily, Max thrust aside the newspaper he had been reading when she had interrupted him with her news about Danny. 'Don't be ridiculous.'

'Girls like that Marcie,' Madge went on self-righteously. 'It's quite obvious that she has an unhealthy hold over him.'

'So he's got a thing about her,' Max said irritably. 'So what? He'll grow out of it.'

Madge was staring at him in disbelief. 'I can't understand you, Max. Your irresponsibility as a parent is

27

appalling.'

'What do you want me to do? Spy on him?'

'If necessary,' Madge said grimly. 'After all, one reads often enough how young people, desperate for money, engage in illegal activities.' She nodded towards the paper Max had been reading.

'Not my kids,' Max said emphatically.

'How can you be sure?'

'Easy. Because unlike your kids, mine come to me when they're in trouble.'

The barb shot home. 'That's unkind.'

'I don't care.' He grabbed up the paper again and made a show of concentrating on it. 'Anything to get it through your thick head that there's no way I'm going to spy on Danny.'

Max waited for a few seconds after she had left the room, then lowered the newspaper. He had to find Danny and have a word with him. He had to get to the bottom of this. He threw the paper onto the floor, and rising to his feet, set out to find his son.

Danny was out in the back yard, puzzling over a couple of the books he needed for his computer course. Max sat down on the grass beside him. 'I want to have a talk with you, mate,' he began. 'But before I start, I want you to know that I trust you. Totally.'

Danny looked momentarily evasive. 'What have I done wrong now?'

'Nothing,' Max hastily assured him. 'But ... ah ... your Aunt Madge, she was cleaning up after you, and she found a whole lot of money in your wallet. Two hundred bucks, she said.'

Danny was outraged. 'She's got no *right* to go snooping in my wallet.'

'Couldn't agree more,' Max said sympathetically. 'But that never stopped Madge, and it probably never will. So how about it – where did you get the money?'

28

'I'm allowed to have money, aren't I?' Now Danny was on the defensive.

'Sure you are. But I'd like to know where it came from. Let's face it, after you've paid for your board, there's no way you'd have that much left out of your pay. I know the bank doesn't pay you so much.'

Danny was staring sullenly down the length of the yard. 'You just said you trusted me.'

'I do,' Max told him. 'But I also know you're hiding something, and I wish you'd tell me what it is.'

Danny hesitated. 'Promise you won't get mad?' he said at last.

'I'll try not to.'

Danny hesitated some more, then apparently coming to a decision, nodded. 'A bloke at work follows the horses a bit. He knew I needed money, so he gave me a tip. It won.'

Max stared at him in surprise. 'You mean you won it *gambling*?'

'I knew you'd be mad,' Danny said with a resigned shrug.

But Max was too relieved to be mad. 'Well, I'd rather you *didn't* gamble – but it's your life.' He pushed himself up onto his feet. 'Thanks for telling me the truth. I appreciate it.'

Danny smiled up at him. 'No worries. Any time.'

Max began to move back towards the house. He stopped and turned back. 'What was the name of the horse?'

'Ah . . .' Danny thought for a moment. 'King Chicken.'

Max nodded and headed once more to the house, quite satisfied with the way the discussion had gone.

He had just entered the house through the back door when the phone began to ring. He reached it a second or two before Madge who came running from the other direction. She watched him with apprehension as he tried to fathom what the guy at the other end of the line was telling him. Something about gorillas. How much did he charge for a gorilla? It had to be some sort of a loony.

'What do you mean, how much do I charge for a gorilla? Now, you listen to me, pal, you ring here again and I'll do you.' He slammed down the receiver.

'It must have been a wrong number,' Madge observed.

Max looked at her. A suspicion began to form. 'I bet it wasn't,' he said slowly. 'I bet that Clive Gibbons was behind it. He got one of his friends to ring me up and annoy me.'

'Oh, I shouldn't think so,' Madge said, a little nervously. 'Why would he do that?'

Max's feeling of goodwill after the interview with Danny had been short lived. That Clive Gibbons... 'I'm going over there right now to find out,' he growled. 'This time he's not going to get away with it.' With his head lowered belligerently, his arms held a little out from his sides, he headed for the door.

'Er... no, Max, don't do that.'

'Why not?' Max stopped and glowered at her. 'He's had it coming for a long time.'

Madge was looking very unhappy. 'Because... ah... that call... it was for me.' She took a deep breath. 'You see, I've been working for Clive... taking calls for his Animalgrams.'

She might as well have taken a knife and driven it straight into his heart. 'You *what*? On *my* phone?'

'Yes, as it happens. It's the only phone here.'

It was another betrayal, another body blow. Max was mentally reeling. 'I don't know how you could, Madge,' he said in a pained voice. 'Not for that moron.'

'Very easily.' Madge was quickly recovering her composure. 'As it happens, I enjoy it. Clive doesn't have a phone installed yet in his house. He asked me if I would do it. He's paying me.'

'I don't care.' Max dismissed this with a curt wave of his hand. 'It's got to stop – is that clear?'

'I'll stop when I feel like it,' Madge returned defiantly, 'and that doesn't happen to be now.'

'You'll do what I tell you,' Max blustered, but it seemed to have no effect on his sister.

'Don't threaten me, Max,' she said evenly. 'I'll do what I like in this house. After all, I *do* own it.'

Max was speechless. There was nothing he could say to that. It was the absolute truth.

The only bright spot on the horizon was the wedding between Des Clarke and Daphne Lawrence who shared the house on the other side of the Robinsons' place. Max had been asked to give the bride away, even if it did mean getting into his best and only suit, the one in which he himself had been married and was now a little too tight for him. But he was taking the responsibility very seriously. He also hoped that it would work out this time for Des who had been stood up four times before by his prospective brides on the eve of the wedding. There was no reason why he should have to be stood up for a fifth time ... but with Des's luck, one never knew. Everyone had their fingers crossed.

On the morning of the wedding, as luck would have it, Max was called out urgently to fix a broken water pipe, with the result that when he finally returned home, there was a great rush to get ready. They had to pick up Daphne and her bridesmaid and get them to the church in time. Shane would be driving them in the company limousine which he had unofficially borrowed for the occasion.

When Max arrived home, Shane was ironing their shirts. 'Madge was supposed to do that,' Max said.

'Where is she, by the way?'

'Dunno.' Shane shrugged. 'Some guy rang. She grabbed her purse and ran off.'

Annoying as this was, there was no time to bother about it. 'I'd better have a quick bath,' Max said, moving out into the passage.

When he emerged from the bathroom about fifteen minutes later, he saw, to his irritation, that Clive Gibbons was in the kitchen, talking to Danny who looked up with a rather guilty expression as Max, still only half-dressed, entered the room. 'Hi, Mr Ramsay,' Clive greeted him brightly. 'Lovely day, isn't it?'

'Depends,' Max grunted. 'Suddenly I detect a bit of a smell.'

'Dad . . .'

'A bad smell, as a matter of fact. Real nasty.'

'Clive's just visiting, Dad,' Danny explained.

'That's right,' Clive said with a quick glance at Danny. 'I dropped in to see Danny.'

'What about?' Max asked suspiciously.

'Ah . . .' Clive looked uneasy.

'He came to borrow a cup of sugar,' Danny supplied hastily, 'and I was about to do the neighbourly thing by giving it to him.'

'Yeah?' Max eyed them both doubtfully. There was *something* going on between them that didn't quite meet the eye. But there was no time to worry about that now; he had to get ready for the wedding at which he had agreed to give the bride away. 'Then after you've given it to him,' he said, 'you can bring a cup of tea to my room.

Shane was waiting beside the limousine when Max finally emerged from the house. There was no sign of Danny. 'Where's Danny?'

'Ah . . .' Now it was Shane's turn to be hesitant. 'He went on ahead.'

'Oh, all right then.' Max began to walk towards the

Clarke house where the bride would be waiting for them. 'Come on, let's go and pick up the bride.'

Daphne was ready. She looked radiant and Max told her so. There was a time, when she had first moved into the street, that he hadn't approved of her. The girl was a stripper, and that was something else that, in his eyes, had given the street a bad name. Now she was a bride; that was perfectly respectable. With her friend, Zoe, the bridesmaid, in tow, they headed for the limousine. Daphne was carrying a bouquet of small red and white flowers.

As they drove through the quiet surburban streets towards the church where the groom would be nervously waiting for them, and perhaps even wondering about the possibility of him being left in the lurch for a fifth time, Max told one of his favourite wedding stories about his father. He sat in the corner of the back seat next to Zoe and the bride, feeling quite expansive. He rather liked weddings.

'... so then in this borrowed suit of this friend of his who was smaller than himself – it was quite okay apparently as long as he didn't bend over or move his arms about too much...'

The car drove smoothly along the quiet streets, its engine making hardly a sound. Daphne clutched her bouquet. 'What happened?' she asked.

'Well, he was about to slip the ring on my mother's finger, but he was nervous and dropped it.'

'Don't tell me...'

'That's right.' Max nodded. 'He bent down to pick it up...'

'How awful,' Zoe exclaimed.

'He was wearing his bright red underpants,' Max told them. 'My mother never forgave him.'

'Every time I hear that story,' Shane said drily from the front seat, 'it gets a little bit more over the top.'

33

'Shane,' Max said in a tone of mock-reproach, 'that's something you've got to learn. You don't want to spoil a good story because of the facts.' He chuckled quite contentedly at his own joke.

'Oh no,' Shane said in dismay. 'I should have known something like this would happen.'

The car was slowing down. 'What's up?' Daphne asked.

'Yes, why are you slowing down?' Max demanded. 'What's the matter?'

Shane gestured towards the street ahead of them. 'Danny. That's what the matter is.'

Danny? Sitting forward, Max peered through the windscreen at the street ahead of them. He couldn't see Danny. All he could see were parked cars, houses and gardens, and ... and ... no, it was impossible ... a gorilla standing by the side of the road, flagging down the car. Max's mouth fell open. All he could do was stare in dumb amazement as the car pulled up beside the hitch-hiking primate, and, reaching across the seat, Shane opened the passenger's door. 'Get in,' he said tightly. The gorilla got in. 'I thought Clive was going to drop you at the church after you finished the job.'

'Clive?' Max exclaimed angrily. 'I *knew* you two were up to something.'

'I hope you don't think you're coming to my wedding dressed like that,' Daphne said tartly. 'This is supposed to be the happiest day of my life.'

'It's perfectly weird,' Zoe remarked.

'What happened to Clive, anyway?' Shane demanded.

'Shut up!' the gorilla muttered in a voice that didn't sound like Danny's.

'Danny?' Shane was looking at the ape curiously.

The man in the gorilla suit started shouting. 'Look, I don't know what you lot are on about, but if you don't shut up I'll blow your brains out.'

That was when they saw the gun in the animal's paw. 'If this is some sort of joke, mate,' Max said reproachfully, 'then it's in pretty poor taste. Now why don't you just get lost and we'll forget all about it.'

'Yes.' Daphne was sitting forward with a murderous expression. 'If you spoil things for me today, I'll ... I'll murder you.' Zoe placed a restraining hand on her arm.

'How many times have I got to tell you?' The gorilla was clearly very agitated. He kept waving the gun about. 'This is no joke.'

'But don't you understand?' Shane was watching the stranger with the gun warily. 'We're on our way to a wedding.' He jerked his head towards Daphne in the back seat. 'She's the bride.'

'And you wouldn't want us to be late, would you?' Zoe said in a small voice.

'What do you want with us, anyway?' Max asked.

'Belt up, will you,' the stranger snarled. 'I've got enough on my plate without you all rabbiting on.' His voice was jerky, barely under control.

'Look, be reasonable,' Shane said evenly. 'Tell us what you want. If we can help you, then we will. If not, then at least we can get on our way.'

'Why does this have to happen to me?' the ape man moaned. 'Everything's going wrong today.'

'I know the feeling,' Daphne remarked.

The ape's face turned to Shane. 'Okay, start the car,' he commanded. 'Let's get moving.'

Shane glanced back at the others. The gun came up to point at his head. Shane started the car. 'Where are we going?'

'Never you mind. Straight ahead for the time being.'

'Is that to the loony bin or to the zoo?' Max couldn't resist it, then recoiled as he found himself staring straight down the barrel of the gun.

'I'm warning you.'

35

'All right, all right.' Max gestured reassuringly, as the ape man turned to face the front again. 'All right. Keep your hair on.' He flinched as once again he found himself looking down the barrel of the gun that was being held in one furry paw.

They drove in silence for about twenty minutes. They had left the suburbs behind and had turned on to a country road when their hijacker ordered Shane to stop the car. Then, brandishing his gun, he ran around to the driver's side. It was already noon; the wedding service was due to start. The ape man gestured wildly with his gun. 'Come on, get out. Right now. Move it.'

Slowly, despondently, they climbed out of the car. 'You can't leave us here,' Zoe protested.

'How are we supposed to get back?' Shane asked.

'What about my wedding?' Daphne was still clutching her bouquet of flowers.

'Who knows, darling?' the stranger said as he climbed in behind the wheel. 'I might be doing you a favour.'

'You . . . you . . .' The others had to restrain Daphne as she lunged forward.

'If I ever see you again,' Shane warned, 'you'd better watch out.'

'But you won't recognise me, will you?' The car sped off down the dusty road.

Mas shook his head. 'A fruitcake,' he muttered. 'A complete and utter fruitcake.'

'Oh, Max,' Daphne wailed. 'What are we going to do?'

Max stared woefully around at the trees and fields and distant mountains. 'Only one thing we *can* do,' he said, taking Daphne's arm. 'Start walking. Come on, love.'

By the time they reached the church, after walking for miles, then flagging down a car driven by an old man 'quick, quick, there's a dangerous gorilla on the loose,' Max had cried to the driver, urging him in a direction quite different from the one he had been taking,

36

everyone had gone home. The bridegroom, quite certain he had been jilted for the fifth time, had been the first to leave. He had disappeared and no one could find him. It was a major upset; the whole neighbourhood was talking about it.

When Shane reported the theft of the limousine to the police, they decided that that particular gorilla must have been one of three who had held up the Wharfdale bank that morning. They questioned him extensively and he came home in a sombre mood.

'Did you get a good look at the man?' Madge asked him on his return.

'Hairy. Just your ordinary gorilla.'

'And he seemed such a nice person,' Madge mused.

Max, who had changed out of his suit, thought she was referring to the missing bridegroom. 'If you ask me, all he's fit for is running out of town on a rail,' he said disgustedly. 'There's got to be something wrong with a bloke who runs away from someone as pretty and as genuine as Daphne.'

Madge was looking at him curiously. 'Max, did *you* get a good look at the gorilla?'

'Yes, I did,' Max answered with feeling. 'And if he hadn't waved that gun about so much, I would have clobbered him good and proper.'

'Gun?' Madge's eyes widened. 'How did he get into the car?'

'I thought it was Danny,' Shane told her.

'Danny?'

'You still haven't told me why,' Max gruffly pointed out to his son.

'He was offered a job.'

'What job?'

'Well, I guess you're going to find out, anyway,' Shane said unhappily. 'Danny works part time for Clive Gibbons, delivering Animalgrams.'

'What?' Madge exclaimed, while Max could feel the blood rushing to his head again. Another one below the belt. How many more of these blows could he take?

'That moron next door,' he groaned.

'I warned Danny about being late for the wedding,' Shane said, 'and when I saw that gorilla hitching a lift, I thought it was him. Naturally. There wouldn't be too many gorillas running around at that time of the day.'

Max didn't know; he didn't know anything any more; the neighbourhood could be infested with gorillas for all he knew, delivering messages and robbing banks. 'That Clive Gibbons,' he fumed. 'I'll give *him* a message he'll never forget.' He thought of something. 'And that chicken who broke into the house that night. Was that . . . ?'

Shane nodded. 'Danny. Yes. He left his clothes in Clive's house while he went out to do a job. When he got back the house was locked. Clive wasn't there. Danny couldn't change back into his own clothes.'

'That Clive Gibbons,' Max muttered again, threateningly. There was a knock at the front door. 'If that's him . . .' Max headed for the door, prepared to do battle.

But it wasn't Clive Gibbons who faced him on the doorstep; it was a rangy gentleman in ill-fitting clothes who introduced himself as Sergeant Harris of B Division. Suddenly apprehensive, Max invited him inside; he had little choice. 'Is this your wife, Mr Ramsay?' the policeman asked when he saw Madge who was now looking very worried.

'No way,' Max replied emphatically. 'She's my sister.'

Harris nodded good-naturedly to Madge, then turned to Max and Shane. 'I heard some garbled story down at the station about a gorilla hijacking your car on the way to a wedding.'

'I've already told them everything I could,' Shane muttered defensively.

'Yes. I'm really here about Danny Ramsay.' The policeman looked hard at Max. 'Your other son. To your knowledge, does he ever wear a gorilla suit?'

'Yes,' Max replied uncomfortably. 'But I've only just found that out.'

'You can't think the bank robber was *Danny*,' Shane protested.

Max laughed; it was too ludicrous to think that the bank robber could be Danny. 'You'd have to be joking. Danny wouldn't do a thing like that.'

'That remains to be seen,' the sergeant said implacably.

Max's smile faded. 'You can ask him yourself when he comes in,' he said tersely.

'He won't be coming in, Mister Ramsay,' Harris said with an engaging smile. 'He's down at the station with your neighbour.'

'Clive Gibbons?' Madge cried out in alarm.

'Correct.' Harris nodded. 'When he and Danny were detained, Mr Gibbons was dressed as a chicken.'

Max's hands were suddenly itching to get around the scrawny neck of that choice item of poultry. Apes and chickens, and a missing bridegroom. And now Danny had been picked up in mistake for one of the other gorillas who had robbed a bank. The world was falling apart. Ramsay Street would never recover.

Two

From the car, Helen Daniels stared across the grass at the tall, distinguished looking man who had just kissed a woman beside the fountain, and sighed. Yes, that was him; that was Douglas Blake; there was no mistake.

He had been waiting beside the fountain as he did every day at this time, according to the private detective she had hired to trace him. It was here that he met a woman with whom he seemed to be on very close terms. He was staying at the nearby Regal Hotel. The private detective had done his job well, working mainly from the sketch Helen had been able to provide him.

She had watched him as he waited by the fountain, glancing every now and again at his wristwatch, then, as the well-dressed woman had walked towards him through the park, he had walked along the path to meet her. He had kissed her in a way that suggested more than mere familiarity. 'Helen, he looks *very* respectable,' Madge Mitchell observed in a tone of disbelief.

'I thought so, too,' Helen said quietly. 'Once.'

Once... They had made such plans; she had really loved him... 'What are you going to do?' Madge asked.

'I'm going to make him pay,' Helen said bitterly, still watching the couple as they walked away from the fountain in the park, arm in arm. Of course he would be exuding perfect charm and sincerity; it was so characteristic of him. 'He's going to pay for everything.' For the money he had swindled out of her, for playing so

40

callously on her emotions. Oh, she had been such a fool. Yes, he would pay.

She had asked Madge to come with her; she had been nervous. If he didn't show up, she had told Madge she would cut her losses and buy her lunch. But then he *had* turned up as the private detective had assured her he would.

'He told me he was an art dealer, and I believed him.' He had promised to stage an exhibition of Helen's paintings. Together, they had picked out a dream cottage in the country to buy.

'I wanted to believe him.' She sighed again then smiled wanly. 'There's no fool like an old fool, I guess.'

They were still watching the couple as they walked along the path, Douglas Blake's head bent attentively towards his female companion. 'How much money was involved?' Madge asked.

'Fifty thousand.' Her savings, and the money Jim had advanced them as an interest-free loan.

'Fifty...' Madge whistled softly. 'Go to the police.'

Helen shook her head. 'Too risky. If he suspects anything, he'll disappear – the way he did before.' She had spent enough money to have him traced, but now, having come this far...

'That woman he's with now – she may be an accomplice, but it's more likely that she's another victim.'

'Helen, you didn't come out here to do *nothing*.'

But what *could* she do? 'I can't even follow him. He'll recognise me.'

'But he doesn't know *me*...'

Helen looked at her speculatively. That was very true.

'I still say you should go to the police,' Madge said after Helen had dropped her back at the Ramsay house and they were settling down to a cup of tea. 'Let them investigate the man.'

41

'I really thought I cared for him, Madge,' Helen said reflectively as she sipped her tea. 'That was the real twist of the knife. I thought I was safe from that kind of emotion. But he made a complete fool of me. I *could* go to the police, of course – perhaps they would even have enough evidence against him to lay charges – but that kind of revenge isn't enough. I want Jim's money back. I have to fool him the way he fooled me.'

'You can't manage that by yourself,' Madge pointed out.

'I know.'

'So what are friends for?'

They looked at each other. Helen's mind was ticking over. It had been ticking over from the moment Madge had pointed out to her that she was unknown to Douglas Blake. But Helen hadn't really intended to involve Madge in this; she had enough troubles of her own, her husband having left her for a younger woman, her son in gaol and not wanting to see her, and of course that impossible brother of hers. She was someone, Helen had always felt, who meant well although her boisterous manner could sometimes fray the nerves. But if she really *did* want to help... 'Thanks, Madge,' she said warmly. 'I *do* have an idea, but it needs developing. I'll come back to you with it, and see what you think.'

It wasn't such a difficult plan; all it would need was sufficient nerve to carry it through – and Helen was quite certain that nerve was one quality Madge possessed in abundance. The plan Helen devised would also require a certain outlay of money which presented no real problem as Helen had just sold one of her paintings for a considerable sum; and in any event, if the plan did succeed – and Helen was sure it would – the returns would be such as to more than fully justify the expense.

Another factor that made Madge ideal for the job was that she was attractive – just the sort, Helen thought, who would catch the eye of a smooth operator like Douglas Blake – and sure enough, Madge reported to her on the day after she had booked into the Regal Hotel, she had been aware of him watching her speculatively from the other side of the dim and rather noisy cocktail bar as she had a drink on that very first night, to all intents and purposes a woman very much alone. The next time Madge called it was to tell a pleased Helen that Douglas Blake had struck up a casual conversation with her in the hotel foyer. He had asked her how long she was staying at the hotel. The fish was already nibbling at the bait.

That accomplished, Madge's next move was to establish herself as a woman of means in a not too obvious way. This she did by complaining to reception about the unsuitability of her room, having made sure that Douglas Blake, reading his newpaper in the foyer, was within earshot. The room, she said distinctly, was far too small for her. Didn't they have anything larger? Well, she was told regretfully, there was only the Presidential Suite available – but of course that was very expensive. Madge wasn't concerned with the expense; the Presidential Suite would do nicely.

It was Douglas Blake who made the next move, accidentally bumping into her as she turned away from the reception desk. He apologised most profusely, and offered to take her to lunch. Madge told him she was about to visit her jewellers. Dinner then? Dinner would be fine. They arranged to meet in the cocktail bar that evening. Madge happily reported all this to Helen who couldn't have been more pleased with the way things were going.

'Have you been to the bank?' she asked.

Madge held out her hand to display the ring that sparkled on her finger. Helen admired it. 'Madge, it's beautiful.'

'I'm not too happy about having the stone removed, I

must admit,' Madge said.

Impulsively, Helen grasped Madge's hand. 'I wouldn't want you to do anything you don't want to do,' she said earnestly. 'If you want to back out, I'll quite understand.'

'No.' Madge smiled and shook her head. 'If you're willing, then so am I.' Helen squeezed her hand in gratitude. 'I just hope I don't lose my nerve, that's all.'

'You won't,' Helen assured her. 'The diamond will say everything for you. The moment Douglas sees it, he's ours.'

The dinner couldn't have been more successful. They had veal; the wine was French and expensive. Douglas Blake – he was calling himself Douglas Manning now – talked about antiques and fine arts, a passion that went right back to his childhood, even surviving the time when his wife died and he thought he would be unable to go on. Madge listened to him sympathetically. Douglas then told her of his great love for jewellery, which Madge assured him she shared. In fact, she said, her husband had bought her several beautiful stones, believing she was safer with diamonds than with cash. Douglas was impressed. He would like to see her collection some time, if that wasn't imposing on her. Madge told him that they were in a bank safety deposit box – but, as it so happened, she did have one of the diamonds with her. Later, she told Helen how Douglas's eyes had lit up when she had tipped a large and sparkling diamond from the little cloth bag she had taken from her purse onto the palm of her hand.

Douglas stared at the diamond that winked and sparkled in the palm of Madge's hand. Madge told him that she had nine others like it, suitable compensation, she thought, from a husband who had walked out on her after twenty years of marriage. She sighed. Not that it was always easy, of course. Douglas looked at her. What

44

did she mean? Was she in some sort of trouble Ah . . . no, no, Madge said quickly and unconvincingly; she could manage, really she could. But Douglas had shrewdly picked up her uncertainty. He knew she had the diamonds, but was she somewhat short of cash? Madge showed surprise and some embarrassment at the question. Douglas nodded sympathetically and refilled her glass. If he could help in any way . . . Madge hesitated, then told him, unhappily, she couldn't pay her hotel bill. Now it was Douglas's turn to be surprised. But she had a small fortune in diamonds – couldn't she sell those? No, she couldn't because she was terrified of what her husband would do if he found out. The diamonds were quite useless to her. It was funny, when you came to think of it; she was worth a fortune, yet she had no money. Douglas leaned forward across the table, his eyes brimming with sincerity.

'We'll have to see what we can do about that, won't we?' he said. The trap was nicely set.

The following morning, Douglas found Madge in the hotel coffee shop. He hoped she didn't mind, but he had taken the liberty of mentioning her plight discreetly – no names, of course – to a jeweller friend of his, who would be quite happy to value her diamonds for her. Madge demurred. She didn't know if she could afford to take the risk. Douglas offered to take the diamonds himself, then seeing her unenthusiastic expression, said, of course, he didn't expect her to trust him alone with them, it was only natural that she should be careful – commendable, in fact – but she would be very welcome to come with him to his friend, the jeweller. Madge still demurred. She couldn't, she said; it was too dangerous; she suspected that her husband was having her watched. But . . . if he really was so determined to help her, she could give him the diamond she had with her; she knew he wouldn't run off with it; she prided herself on being a good judge of character. When she told him this, Douglas smiled warmly and reached out for her hand. By her expression, Madge showed him how touched she was by his concern.

The diamond Madge had taken from her ring was worth ten thousand dollars. When Douglas told her that evening that his jeweller friend could sell it easily for five thousand, Madge smiled in what she hoped he would interpret as delight. He had been late, and Madge had almost given way to panic at the thought that she would never see her diamond again. She had called Helen who had urged her to remain calm; he would show up; he wouldn't be satisfied with just the one diamond when he could possibly get his hands on nine others as well. Even so, it had been a tense couple of hours before Douglas finally showed up, full of apologies; the valuation had taken longer than he had expected, he had told her. Madge had been enormously relieved to see her diamond again.

'Five thousand?' Helen said when Madge called her with the news. 'How generous of him. That's almost half its real value.'

'What do we do now, Helen?' Madge queried.

'We continue to twist the knife,' Helen told her with some relish. 'Slowly but surely we twist the knife.'

At the Regal Hotel, Madge was still playing the role of the impoverished, middle-aged divorcee who was unable to pay her bill. Douglas Blake told her not to worry about that; he was only too pleased to help. Madge told him how tremendously grateful to him she was. Her eyes glistened, she choked back an inadvertent sob. She was doing very well.

He asked her again why on earth, if she really was in such dire straits, she didn't sell her diamonds. Because, strictly speaking, she told him, they still belonged to her husband, who had given them to her in the full knowledge that she wouldn't be able to sell them without his co-operation. Douglas looked thoughtful. Why would her husband have to know? Because, Madge said, according to plan, he knew just about every gem dealer in the country and had made it clear to them that they would risk losing his custom if they bought any precious stones from her. Her husband was a very influential man. Madge wondered if she sounded convincing enough; she was certainly speaking with enough subdued sincerity.

As she expected, Douglas Blake had a solution. Why didn't Douglas buy the stones himself? He did a little trading in gems from time to time.

Madge feigned wide-eyed amazement, effectively concealing her exhilaration that he was walking blindly into the trap she and Helen had set for him. Marvellous. Not all of them, surely? she asked.

Why not? Douglas was almost certain he could raise the money within twenty-four hours. Of course, Madge protested a little – not too much, but just enough to make it convincing.

'We're getting close, Helen,' Madge said cheerfully later that morning after she had brought Helen up to date on the latest developments. Helen had just put the kettle on for tea. Madge had come breezily into the kitchen with shining eyes and flushed cheeks; she was clearly enjoying her undercover role. 'You know, he's so plausible. I almost found myself believing in him.'

Yes, plausible. Helen was putting out the cups. 'I believed every blasted word he said,' she murmured.

'I'm not at all surprised,' Madge said, 'now that I've met him. You'd have to be almost psychic to see through that act.'

'Perhaps.' Helen leaned back against the sink with her arms folded. 'Where is he now? Seeing his accountant? Arranging finance?' She knew his style; she had already been a victim of it.

'We're getting close, Helen,' Madge said.

'Yes, but he's no fool,' Helen remarked grimly. 'I'm worried he'll sense he's being set up.'

Madge smiled. 'Never.'

Helen smiled back at her. 'Perhaps you should think about a career on the stage when this is over.'

'I might just do that,' Madge laughed. The kettle was boiling. Helen poured the water into the teapot. 'You know, Helen,' Madge said thoughtfully, 'I'm awfully glad we're friends. I'd hate to have you as an enemy.'

'I think Douglas Blake is the first person to have that privilege,' Helen said quietly. 'I've been taken for a fool before, but never that *and* fifty thousand dollars.' She was becoming angry again, just thinking about it.

The frustrating part of it for Helen was having to wait for Madge to keep her informed of what was happening. So many things could go wrong; it was all very tricky. If Douglas Blake got away this time . . . In the meantime, all she could do was wait, with some impatience, for Madge to report to her what was happening between her and Douglas Blake. And when Madge did report, it was a matter of filling in for herself the finer details, such as the winning smile with which Douglas would have informed Madge at lunch that day that he had a definite buyer for her diamonds. They would be drinking champagne of course; it was a time for celebration.

The buyer Douglas had found would purchase Madge's diamonds for fifty thousand dollars – a figure Madge pretended to be utterly delighted with. And then, to allay any doubts Douglas might have had at not being able to see all ten diamonds, Madge confessed rather shamefacedly, as had been arranged, that she hadn't been entirely honest with him. She'd already had the diamonds valued before she met him. She showed him a valuation document which he studied quickly and anxiously. Then with relief he handed it back to her. The diamonds had been valued at four thousand dollars each, according to the document. This, he said, of course, was a pittance; her husband had told her that the jeweller was trying to rob her. Madge wasn't a fool. She smiled across at Douglas as the waiter brought more champagne. Then they raised their glasses to each other; it was so good to be dealing with a man she could trust, she said. Douglas, now accepting the fact that she did indeed have ten diamonds, was delighted to propose a toast to a lady who was shortly to become fifty thousand dollars richer. In her own mind Madge toasted the man who was soon to become fifty thousand dollars poorer.

Douglas had told her he was meeting the buyer that afternoon. Madge would have her money by five at the latest. When she called Helen with the news, Madge said she was feeling like a cat on a hot tin roof. Helen, too, was on edge. 'Are you sure he doesn't suspect anything?'

'Not a thing. The false document from the jeweller worked perfectly. He's convinced there are ten genuine stones.'

'Then you mustn't let your guard down for a second,' Helen warned her. 'Not now. Particularly not now.'

'I won't. Don't worry.'

'Okay. Now remember, after he's given you the money, just leave without any fuss. Walk out of the hotel, get into a taxi and come straight here. Right?'

'Right. He said he'd be back at five.'

'Good,' Helen said. 'Stay calm. A couple more hours and it'll be all over.'

'I'll see you at five-thirty,' Madge promised.

'Good luck.' Helen slowly replaced the receiver. So close, almost in the bag – if nothing went wrong at the last minute. It was hard to believe that this plan of hers was actually going to work. But if anything did go wrong... She had to make sure it didn't. A little extra pressure had to be applied to Douglas Blake. She picked up the receiver again and began to dial.

Helen's phone rang just after four. 'He took the bait, Mrs Daniels,' the caller said. 'I've given him twenty-four hours to hurry him up.'

'That's excellent, Mr Rawlings,' said Helen, hugely relieved. Rawlings was the private detective she had hired to find Douglas.

'I found him in the hotel lobby,' Rawlings went on. I let him know who I was. More importantly, I let him know that I knew who *he* was. I told him I had an appointment with you right at that very place – and believe me, that shook him. I told him that you had hired me to track him down. Some outstanding business matter, I said. I could report his exact whereabouts, but on the other hand the information could take a little while to reach you – say twenty-four hours. A small consideration – five hundred dollars would cover it ... He didn't like that, of course; he put on a bit of an act. But I made him see reason.'

'You've done well, Mr Rawlings.' Helen was delighted it had gone so smoothly. All it had needed was just that little extra pressure. 'We can expect to hear from our Mr Blake soon then?'

'If he's the sort of con I'm used to he'll be making his move quite smartly,' Rawlings said. 'Nothing scares them more than a little heat.'

Everything was falling nicely into place. Helen relished the moment when she would come face to face with Douglas Blake again. Yes, she would be there for the kill.

It was just after five o'clock, and there was no sign of Douglas. From her vantage point in the far corner of the hotel lobby where Douglas had arranged to meet Madge with the money, Helen had the almost panicky feeling that something had gone wrong at the last minute, that Douglas's suspicions had been aroused and he was keeping away. She could see Madge sitting rather tensely on the other side of the lounge. Between them, people came and went, skirting the potted plants; others sat around, and smoking. Helen glanced nervously at her wristwatch. Douglas was already five minutes late.

Then, suddenly, she saw him, threading his way through the crowded lobby from the entrance, tall and distinguished, his black eyebrows knotted in a small frown which cleared when he saw Madge. Helen watched apprehensively as he sat down beside Madge, reached into the breast pocket of his jacket and produced an envelope, which he then handed to her. She then passed him a small velvet bag which she had taken from her purse. With a quick glance around the lobby, he opened the bag and looked quickly inside. Then, with one of his charming smiles, he stood up. Madge also stood up. They shook hands and Madge left, hurrying out through the main entrance. It was now Helen's moment.

Douglas was sauntering towards the cocktail lounge, looking very pleased with himself. 'Douglas,' she called.

He tensed, then spun to face Helen who was gratified by his stricken expression when he saw her. He looked older, more vulnerable. Then the confident smile was back. 'Helen, this *is* a surprise.'

'Yes, isn't it?'

They faced each other. People moved around them. Music was drifting out from the cocktail bar. 'It's been a long time.'

'A long time.'

'And I must say you're looking wonderful.'

All the old charm. Helen could see how nervous he was beneath it. He began to edge away from her. 'I'm

51

feeling wonderful,' Helen said. 'No, don't rush away. There's something I have to tell you.'

They were standing near the flower stall. At the reception desk, people were studying brochures. An airport bus deposited more arrivals. Luggage was carried to the lifts. 'I'm so pleased you were able to meet that rich divorced lady.'

Douglas was glancing nervously around him. 'What do you know about that?'

'Everything.' Helen was enjoying his discomfort. 'Including one fascinating piece of information that even *you* don't know.'

'It was a business deal.' There was a slight beading of perspiration at his hairline. His tongue flicked briefly along his lower lip. 'Fair to both sides.'

'Of course it was,' Helen said evenly. 'What could be fairer? Fifty thousand for one hundred thousand dollars worth of diamonds might have seemed just the tiniest bit one-sided – but fifty thousand for fakes? I'd say that's generous to the extreme.'

'Fakes?' Douglas's mouth fell open. Reaching into his pocket, he brought out the small velvet bag Madge had given him. He opened the bag and stared at the stones in mounting horror.

'Very good fakes,' Helen told him. 'But I can assure you that they're one hundred per cent glass. I'm afraid, Douglas,' she went on pleasantly, 'that you've been taken in.' He was stunned. He stared at her. He looked even older. 'I've been waiting a long time for this, Douglas,' Helen continued relentlessly. 'You deceived me financially and emotionally. I suggest you think twice from now on before you cheat anybody else.' She had said enough; she had made her point. She was about to turn away when she stopped to deliver a parting blow. 'There was a time, Douglas, when I would have trusted you with everything I had. But now . . . now I can only pity you.'

She walked briskly towards the hotel entrance beyond which people were still stepping down from the airport bus.

Three

The last passenger to step down from the bus was a girl in shorts with a pack on her back. Jim Robinson, by now quite concerned, swung up into the doorway to check inside the bus. But there was no one left. Scott was definitely not on the bus.

'Where is he, Dad?' Lucy wanted to know as he stepped back down onto the pavement. 'Where's Scott?'

Jim wished he knew; it was all very worrying. It had been strange enough that the school excursion tour had been cut short in the first place. Scott hadn't said anything on the telephone; all he had said was that the tour had been cut short and that he would be returning that afternoon. He had told his father what time the bus would be arriving. But he wasn't on that bus. There was always the possibility, of course, Jim thought, that Scott had called home while he and Lucy were waiting at the terminal for the bus to arrive.

But he hadn't, Jim discovered on returning to the house. 'There must be some mistake,' Helen said. 'What time is the next bus?'

Jim had checked. 'There isn't one.'

'He might have let us know.'

'I'll call the school.'

But there was no reply when Jim dialled the school number. He tried the parents of one of the other boys who had gone on the excursion. Yes, he learned the trip had been cut short. There was nothing official as yet, he

54

reported to his mother-in-law after he had finished the call. 'There's talk that some of the boys were playing up.'

Helen came to her grandson's defence. 'Scott wouldn't have been involved in that,' she stated.

Jim frowned worriedly. 'It must have been something pretty serious if the teachers felt that the trip had to be cut short.'

'I can't understand why the school hasn't been in touch with the parents,' Helen remarked.

Paul, Jim's elder son, was unconcerned. 'He obviously just missed the bus, that's all.'

'Then why hasn't he phoned?' Jim queried.

Paul shrugged. 'Knowing Scott, he hasn't got any money.'

'It can't be that,' Helen said. 'He knows to ring reverse charges.'

'Anyway, Scott's a big boy now,' Paul observed off-handedly. 'He can look after himself.'

'I don't know . . .' Helen was giving voice to Jim's own doubts. 'There's something about this, Jim. I can feel it in my bones.'

In the morning, when he called the school, Jim was told some very disturbing news by the principal. Scott had disappeared – and there was a very good reason for his disappearance. He had been accused of rape. Jim was stunned by the news.

Helen was just as stunned. 'I don't understand why the school didn't contact us immediately,' she said, turning away from the canvas on which she had been working.

'I assume they wanted to be sure of their facts,' Jim suggested unhappily. 'The principal is waiting for the full story when they get back. When Scott ran away, it was assumed he would come straight home.'

'From his telephone call that was obviously what he intended to do,' Helen said. 'But he never made it to the

55

bus.' She stared fearfully at her son-in-law. 'He must have had an accident, Jim.'

'Not necessarily,' Jim pointed out to her. 'Maybe he needs some time to work things out. *We* know he would never be involved in anything like that. Maybe he's trying to prove it to other people.'

'All the same...' Helen's eyes were brimming; she had gone quite pale. 'I wish he would come home. We could help him then.' She shook her head sorrowfully. 'He's probably terrified.'

So far the police weren't involved, Jim had been informed by the school principal. But if Scott didn't turn up soon they would have to be called in, and then the story would come out. Perhaps, Jim thought, some of Scott's friends who were also on the trip might be able to help. But he didn't know who Scott's friends were; the boy tended to be something of a loner.

Helen didn't really know, either, when he asked her. 'What about Mike Young?' she suggested after some moments' consideration. 'You know – the boy in the coffee shop. He's in Scott's year.'

Jim nodded. It was a place to start.

Mike Young had heard about the trouble on the school excursion; in fact, the whole school was talking about it. 'I want to talk to some of the boys who were there,' Jim told him. 'The ones Scott would have known best.'

Mike looked doubtful. 'I don't know, Mr Robinson. They mightn't want to get involved.'

They were sitting at one of the tables towards the rear of the almost deserted coffee shop. 'I only want to know if they have any idea where Scott might have gone,' Jim said earnestly. 'His grandmother and I are frankly very worried.'

'It's not surprising he took off,' Mike said. 'I heard about the rape charge.'

Jim could feel his anger rising. If the word about this had spread so quickly . . . 'There *isn't* a charge of rape,' he tersely reminded the boy. 'The police haven't been brought into it. But Scott ran away before he knew that.' Sitting forward, his arms on the table, his hands clasped together, he spoke quietly but intensely. 'I've *got* to find him, Mike. I've got to make sure he's all right. And to give him a chance to explain what really happened.'

'Gee, I didn't know.' Mike regarded him with a worried expression. 'Okay then. I'll try and find out who his best mates are, and get them to contact you.'

'Thanks, Mike. I appreciate that.' Unclasping his hands, Jim pushed his chair back and stood up. Mike also rose to his feet. 'Will you do that as soon as you can?'

'The minute I get back to school,' Mike promised him.

'Thanks, Mike,' Jim said again. 'Then maybe if I came down again this evening . . . ?'

'Sure thing, Mr Robinson. Although I can't promise anything.'

When Mike saw him again that evening, Mike's news was discouraging. 'Nobody knows where Scott is,' he said. 'He just shot through.'

Jim tried not to show his disappointment. 'Someone must know *something*.'

'The kids don't want to talk about it.'

This time they were in the kitchen. Mike was slicing tomatoes. Jim watched him. 'Are you sure?'

Mike looked up at him. 'Well . . . the three kids who were with Scott that night are back now. I just *might* be able to get them to talk to you . . .'

'When?' Jim asked eagerly. 'Tonight?'

Mike picked up another tomato. 'Maybe tomorrow morning. I'll have a word with them. But I can't promise they'll have anything to say.'

'They can talk to me in strict confidence,' Jim assured him. 'All I want to do is locate Scott.'

Mike frowned down at the tomato he had just finished slicing. 'All right,' he murmured. 'I'll try and get them to go to your place.'

Later that evening, Jim received a telephone call from Mike. He had spoken to the three guys he had mentioned to Jim. He had passed on Jim's promise that whatever they said would be treated in confidence – and after some argument and considerable persuasion on Mike's part, they had finally agreed to come to Jim's place first thing in the morning.

The following morning, after a restless night, Jim waited impatiently for the three boys to arrive. There had still been no word from Scott. He prowled through the house; he kept glancing at his wristwatch; he made tea. Finally, the doorbell rang. Jim almost ran along the hall in his haste to open it.

The three boys looked nervous. Jim invited them to sit down. Two of them sat awkwardly at each end of the couch; the third, adopting an attitude of cockiness that Jim could tell was more than a little forced, remained standing. Jim perched on the arm of the chair opposite them. 'Boys, I need to find out what happened on the trip. All I've heard so far are rumours.'

The boys glanced quickly at each other. 'What kind of rumours?' the boy who had remained standing demanded.

'Well, it's very sketchy,' Jim replied, 'and, frankly, it doesn't ring true. All I've heard is that you were at some party or other. Scott took a girl outside. The girl's father turned up and found them together.' That was all Mike had been able to tell him as a result of his enquiries at the school the previous afternoon. 'Now Scott's vanished.' He looked closely at each of them in turn. They were obviously uneasy and avoided his eye. 'So what can you tell me about that? I have to know,' he said when there was no reply. 'I won't repeat anything you tell me – I promise you that.' He looked intently at each of them again. 'Is the story true? Did Scott . . . force himself on the girl?'

'Yeah.' The boy who was on his feet turned towards the door. 'That's what happened, okay?'

The other two boys were on their feet. 'That's *not* what happened,' one of them blurted out. 'Scott never touched her.'

'He would have,' the first boy returned sullenly. 'He wanted to.'

Jim pushed himself up from the arm of the chair. He stared at the third boy. 'Well? What do *you* have to say?'

The boy was looking down at the floor. 'He didn't touch her,' he mumbled.

Jim didn't know who to believe. He tried the second boy. 'Will you tell me exactly what happened?'

'Well, Scott fancied this chick,' the boy said uncomfortably. 'They went outside. We went out, too.'

'Except she took it seriously,' the first boy supplied. 'She got scared.'

'Reckon.' The second boy nodded seriously. 'Then her old man turned up and she screamed rape.'

'She said he'd call the cops.'

'None of us touched her – honest. Scott just bolted.'

'But where is he?' Jim asked.

None of them could tell him. 'Your guess is as good as ours,' the first boy said with a shrug.

He wasn't any nearer to finding out what had happened to his son. Helen insisted he go to the police. 'Not yet,' he said. 'There must be *something* I haven't thought of doing.' He had drawn up a list of names then crossed them out. He had telephoned other parents, none of whom could help him. He felt so helpless.

'You need help, Jim,' Helen said. 'You can only do so much. The police are much better equipped to handle this sort of thing.'

'I don't know...' It was the accusation of rape that worried him.

Helen showed her exasperation. 'Surely, the more people who are looking for him, the stronger our chances are of finding him. The longer you put it off, you know, the more difficult it's going to be to explain to the police.'

She had a point, of course. Jim could see there was really no other way. 'Yes, you're right,' he said resignedly. 'I guess, in a way, I *have* been putting it off.' He became more resolute. 'I'll do it now.' He called the police,

Sergeant Worth was a sympathetic man. He was very experienced in such matters. As he told him when he called at the house later that morning, he knew how trying it was for parents to report missing children. Heck, he had children of his own, and if any of *them* went suddenly missing... He knew how Jim – Helen, too, he added with a sympathetic glance at her – must be feeling at this moment. He would also like them to know from the outset that in the vast majority of cases in which he had been involved over the years, the missing person had turned up safe and sound. 'Both of you can help us a great deal, you know.'

It all sounded very reassuring, but... 'What do you need from us then?'

Worth opened his briefcase and took out a form. He opened his pen. 'I'll need a few details.' He looked up enquiringly. 'Height?'

Jim and Helen frowned at each other. It was different to know exactly. 'Well, he's tall,' Jim said thoughtfully. 'Not as tall as I am, but certainly I think you can say he's above average for his age.'

'Take your time,' the sergeant said. 'I'll need weight, build, complexion, distinguishing marks – scars and so on.' He turned to Helen. 'What sort of clothes would he have been wearing?'

'Oh ... Helen shook her head helplessly. 'He was on a school excursion. I don't know what he would have been wearing.'

'We might have to guess at that,' Worth said, sipping the coffee Helen had made just after he arrived. 'Perhaps you could draw up a list of the things you think he may have taken with him. Oh yes, and would you happen to have a recent photograph?'

'A school photograph, I suppose,' Helen said after thinking about it for a moment. 'It mightn't be terribly good.'

'But something,' the sergeant said. 'At least it would be something.'

Now that it was in the hands of the police, Jim felt only a little better. If there was only something he himself could be doing, instead of all this waiting around to hear news of his son. But there was nothing he could do. He found it impossible to concentrate on his work. He started every time the telephone rang. His hands shook; he was a bundle of nerves. The waiting was a tremendous strain.

At lunch time, Mike Young called with some more information that he had managed to dig out at school. It wasn't much, just that Scott had apparently told one of the kids that he intended to hitch-hike back to the city from where he would catch the bus home. Jim thanked him, then resumed his vigil, while Helen concentrated on the list of clothing Scott would have taken with him on the excursion.

Sergeant Worth returned to the house early that afternoon. When Jim saw him standing on the front doorstep with a rather solemn expression, he immediately feared the worst. He invited the policeman inside.

'Do you recognise this?' Worth produced a soggy wallet and held it out to Jim and Helen who had just put on the jug for coffee. Jim's heart began to beat more rapidly; he was suddenly very frightened.

'It looks very much like Scott's,' he said weakly. The sergeant opened the wallet. Jim stared in dismay at the plastic identity card that bore Scott's name and address. 'Yes, it's his.' He looked at the policeman in fearful enquiry.

Helen took the wallet from Worth. 'It's wet. Where did you find it?'

'In the river.' Worth's expression was impassive. 'On the body of a young man.'

The colour drained from Helen's face. She held the waterlogged wallet protectively between her hands. 'No . . . It can't be.'

'Was it . . . ?' Jim was clasping his own hands together in an effort to stop them trembling. 'Was it Scott?'

'I'm afraid you're the only ones who can tell us that,' Worth said gently. 'He'll need to be formally identified.'

'Of course.'

Worth glanced at Helen. 'Is there anyone who can stay here with Mrs Daniels?'

'My son Paul,' Jim replied.

'Can you get in touch with him?'

'Helen's got his number.'

Helen was obviously in a state of shock. Still clutching Scott's sodden wallet, she was staring blankly ahead of her while the tears streamed down her cheeks. 'I don't think she should be left by herself,' Worth said quietly to Jim. 'Perhaps you should get hold of your son and have him come over here straightaway.'

Half an hour later, Jim was standing on the bank of the river, staring down at the covered body that lay on a plastic sheet near the water's edge. One of the policemen who had been standing near the body when Jim and Sergeant Worth arrived, bent over and carefully drew the cover back from the corpse's face. Jim had steeled himself for this moment. He forced himself to look down at the exposed face. Somewhere on the other side of the river, a bird was singing gaily.

He stared in horror down at the puffy face that had been revealed to him; at the short spiky hair, the half-closed eyes and the distorted mouth. Perplexed, he turned to Worth who was standing slightly behind him. He shook his head. 'That's not him,' he whispered. 'That's not my son.'

'Not Scott?' Helen repeated weakly when he told her the news. 'Oh ... thank God for that.'

'It was some other poor kid.' Paul was still shaken by the experience. 'Somebody's kid.' He sat down heavily on the couch. 'They don't know who he is. And how he happened to have Scott's wallet on him, I have no idea.'

'Stolen?' Helen dabbed at her red-rimmed eyes with a handkerchief.

'Yes, it had to be stolen. But it's how it was stolen that worries me. What they had to do to get the wallet off him.' He had been worrying about that all the way home in the police car.

'Perhaps if we rang around the hospitals,' Helen suggested. Perhaps. Jim didn't know. He just wanted to be alone, that was all.

But that didn't help. Nothing helped. It was not knowing ... That was the awful part of it. If the boy who had been dragged from the river *had* been Scott ... well, at least there would no longer have been any uncertainty about it. They would just have had to learn to live with the fact. It would just have to have been accepted. But this, the not knowing ... It was agony.

The police had come up with nothing. Sergeant Worth tried to be reassuring – but Jim could only think of the worst. Helen was silent, withdrawn; Jim's temper was short. And then the telephone call came, and suddenly everything was different. There was no longer any uncertainty. Scott was alive. He had called from the hospital where he had been laid up for the past two days.

'Oh, my God,' Jim cried out in relief when he heard Scott's voice. 'I never thought I'd hear your voice again.'

'I'm sorry, Dad.' Scott's voice was subdued. He sounded close to tears.

'So where are you, son? I'll come and pick you up.'

Scott was in a small country hospital. It took Jim and Paul more than two hours to drive there. Scott was lying back against the pillows with his eyes closed. He looked pale. There was a small bandage on one side of his forehead.

As they crossed to the side of his bed, Scott's eyes opened, and for a moment he looked startled. 'It's okay, mate,' Paul said as the nurse who had brought them to the room closed the door behind her. 'It's only us.'

Scott's expression relaxed. Jim smiled fondly down at the son he had almost come to believe he would never see again. 'Dad... Paul. Sorry, I'm still a bit jumpy.'

'Take it easy, son.' Jim glanced across at Paul on the other side of the bed. There was a constriction in his throat, a mistiness in his eyes. 'Maybe he should stay here another night.'

'No, Dad. Please.' Scott shook his head. 'I'm fine. I just want to get out of here.'

Jim wasn't convinced; Scott didn't look well at all. Scott stared up at him pleadingly. 'All right, son,' Jim said at last. 'But no rushing around.'

'Anyway, what the hell have you been up to?' Paul demanded. 'Vanishing like that? I was beginning to get scared to open a newspaper in case your stupid face was staring out at me.'

Scott smiled wanly. 'So was I.' Then seeing his father's expression, the smile faded. 'I was trying to get home,' he explained. 'The school safari turned into a disaster.'

'Yes,' Jim said reproachfully. 'The least you could have done was call us.'

'I know,' Scott said ruefully. 'I guess I just panicked. It wasn't as if I had *done* anything.'

'But that girl...'

'She was scared.'

'But she did accuse you.'

'Because my so-called mates scared her,' Scott said. 'The dance was going very well. During one of the breaks she and I went outside for a stroll. Those guys came out after us. They hassled us. They thought it was funny. Anyway, when her dad turned up, she panicked. She told him *we* were attacking her.' He continued to stare up at his father. 'I know I should have stayed, but I didn't want to be accused of something I hadn't done.'

'Well, if it's any comfort to you,' Jim informed him, 'those boys did the right thing in the end. They told me you weren't involved.'

'They're no friends of mine any more,' Scott muttered.

'So you ran away...'

'I was scared the police might be looking for me. So...' Scott lifted one hand slightly from the bed cover then let it drop again... 'I hitched a lift. I was clobbered, my wallet was stolen, I was dumped out of the car, and I ended up here.'

Jim tried not to be too sharp with the boy; it wasn't the time. 'I've warned you about doing silly things like that.'

'I know,' Scott said sheepishly. 'I guess I wasn't thinking too straight.'

'All right,' Jim said. 'We won't worry about that now. The most important thing right now is to get you home.'

Helen had packed a bag with clean clothes for Scott. Paul placed it on the chair beside the bed. 'Here you are. Something for you to change into. It's about time you stopped all this lounging around.' He grinned warmly at his younger brother. 'Some people will do anything to get out of school.'

This time it was a joke that all of them shared.

Four

Gorillagrams and chickengrams – even tap-dancing-grams, to which Clive had once given serious consideration, as he had also given serious consideration to pet rocks, yo-yos, hoola hoops and garden gnomes – were in the past. He had just embarked on a new venture with Shane Ramsay. RAGGS, they called themselves – Ramsay and Gibbons Gardening Services – and they had just landed their first job which, Clive told Shane, would be a lulu. It involved a big house with a large garden which needed landscaping, a swimming pool – and a vision in a swimsuit called Beth Travers. They would be earning fourteen dollars an hour.

It had been time, Clive had said to Shane, for a change, particularly after the fiasco that had led to him and Danny Ramsay being picked up in mistake for the gorillas who had robbed the bank on that fateful day when everything had gone wrong. Another outcome of that particular day of disasters was that Shane had lost his job for allowing one of the bank-robbing primates to hijack his limousine on the way to a wedding when he shouldn't even have been driving it at all. So, with both of them more or less at a loose end, they had agreed to go into business together.

Carrying a folder which contained work orders and plans, Clive led the way importantly down the side of the house towards the terraced area at the rear, while Shane, laden down with a pick, two shovels and a hoe, struggled to keep them from slipping from his grasp. He cannoned into Clive at the corner of the house where he had abruptly stopped. 'There she is,' Clive said, pointing. 'What did I tell you?'

Still juggling his various implements, Shane stared at the vision in the very skimpy two-piece swimsuit who was lying on a reclining chair beside the pool. Her skin was tanned, her long hair honey blonde. She was wearing large round sunglasses. 'Just remember,' Clive said, 'I do all the talking.' He stepped forward out onto the terrace. 'Hello there, Mrs Travers,' he called, smiling broadly.

The woman stirred on the chair. She dangled one leg over the side and pushed the sunglasses up onto her forehead. She smiled. 'Hello, Clive.'

'I'll be with you in a moment, Mrs Travers. I just have to issue a few orders to my man here.' Shane's jaw set grimly. He glared at Clive who had turned back to face him. 'Leave that stuff down there,' Clive said, pointing down beyond the pool, and loud enough for the young, woman on the reclining chair to hear. 'Then you can get the rest of the gear out of the van.'

'Hang on,' Shane said through gritted teeth. 'Just what *is* this?'

Clive studied him blandly. 'Something wrong?'

'What's all this "do this" and "do that" number? It's a partnership – remember?'

Clive glanced quickly over his shoulder at the barely covered woman beside the pool. 'Keep your voice down. Of course, it's a partnership. I'm putting in my organisational ability at the moment while you supply the brawn.'

'One of these shovels is for you.'

'As soon as Beth and I have settled on the plans,' Clive smoothly assured him, 'I'll be in there working, don't you worry. Now go on, put that stuff over there.'

Shane scowled at him, then grudgingly carried the

tools across the terrace to the spot Clive had indicated, while Clive himself joined the young woman beside the pool. 'Ah, workmen,' Shane heard him say in disapproval. 'You know what they're like.' Shane could easily have hit him over the head right then with one of the shovels. Instead, he let the tools drop onto the ground.

'May I?' Clive indicated the lower end of the reclining chair.

'Yes, certainly.' Beth Travers shifted to make room for him.

When he was seated, Clive opened his folder. 'Now I've made a few preliminary sketches. You might like to peruse them.'

'Yes, of course.' She sounded impressed. Clive passed her the sketches. She studied them while Shane studied Clive, who, with a self-satisfied smirk, was sitting very close to the woman. 'Oh, I like that.' She pointed to one of the sketches.

'Mmmm?' To Shane it was apparent that Clive was more interested in the woman than in the sketch. 'Which?'

Her finger moved. Her skin was like burnished gold in the sunlight. 'Those squiggly lines there.'

'That's a ti-tree fence.' Shane could almost see him swelling with pride. 'I thought for privacy, and . . .'

'Oh yes, privacy. That's very important.'

'Well, you never know,' Clive said suggestively. 'If you ever feel like sunbathing, completely, as it were . . .'

'And the dots?' Beth was pointing again. 'They look as though they might be interesting.'

Clive looked. 'Frangipani trees.'

'Oh yes. I like that.'

'Yes. I asked myself, what could be nicer than a day by the pool, the warmth of the sun – and the subtle perfume of frangipani wafting on a gentle breeze?'

'Yes, I *do* like that. I think it's a wonderful idea.'

Shane had heard enough of this. 'Clive,' he called. 'Come here.'

The warm and friendly smile disappeared from Clive's face as he looked across at Shane. Then, with a sigh, he pushed himself from his end of the reclining chair. 'Excuse me, Mrs Travers.'

'Beth.'

'Beth.' Clive beamed down at the exposed cleavage.

'Clive,' Shane called again, impatiently.

Scowling, Clive stalked across the flagged terrace towards him. 'What's wrong with you?' he growled.

'If you think I'm going to do this whole job on my own,' Shane told him tersely, 'while you carry on over there, you're wrong, buddy.'

'Don't stress yourself,' Clive said. 'I only need a few minutes more.'

He returned to the reclining chair on which Beth Travers was once more lying full length. Fuming, Shane heard him say, apologetically, 'I have to be careful. He does a bit of a bad back routine sometimes.'

'Oh dear.' Beth turned her head towards Shane. 'Should he be doing hard work then?'

'It's all in his mind,' Clive carelessly informed her. 'He was a champion diver once, but hurt his back one day while he was training. But it's really only psychological now.'

Shane had taken off his shirt. 'He certainly still *looks* like an athlete,' Beth observed with a touch of admiration.

'Yes, it's a pity they go to flab so quickly,' Clive hurriedly pointed out. 'But I do most of the work. It helps him keep his dignity.'

He was lying through his teeth. Angrily, Shane picked up one of the shovels. 'Phew, it's awfully hot,' Beth remarked, sitting up again on the chair. 'I'll get us something to drink. Some lemonade.'

Clive smiled at her winningly. 'That would be very nice, Beth,' he said. 'That's very thoughtful of you. Ta very much.'

Beth Travers walked back to the house with a slow but insolent swing of her hips. Clive stared after her, his expression full of longing. He sighed. Shane began to dig.

Pausing only to drink the lemonade Beth had handed him with a bewitching smile, Shane continued to dig the hole while, to his utter disgust, Clive sat at the table beside the pool beneath a striped umbrella, sipping his lemonade and chatting companionably to Beth Travers opposite him. The mound of dirt beside Shane grew larger. It was a hot day; the sweat was streaming down his body as he worked. 'Then, of course, there's Rio,' Clive said.

It seemed that Beth's thoughts were elsewhere. 'What was that? she asked distantly. From behind her outsized sunglasses, she was staring in Shane's direction.

'Rio.'

'Oh, yes. Mardi Gras.'

'Very lively. A stunning spectacle.' But she still wasn't paying him any attention. Following the direction of her speculative gaze, Clive turned his head towards Shane. 'That's deep enough, Shane,' he called. Shane stopped digging, and taking a crumpled handkerchief from his shorts, dabbed his glistening face with it as he leaned wearily on the shovel. 'We want the ditch longer. Okay? Make it longer.'

'He should rest for a while,' Beth said solicitously. 'It's so hot.'

'No, he's okay.' He leaned forward confidentially across the table. 'Now take Mexico.' He pronounced it 'Mehico'. 'The home of the tacos and the tortilla...'

Ignoring him, Beth called to Shane. 'Why don't you

cool off in the pool?' she suggested.

Shane thought that was a terrific idea. 'Thanks. I will.' Dropping the shovel, he sauntered across to the side of the pool. Beth stood up, and taking off her sunglasses, laid them on the table. 'Will you join us?' she asked Clive.

'Ah . . .' Clive was suddenly hesitant. 'Not today. I have to work on the plans.'

Shane dived effortlessly into the pool. His body neatly cleaved the refreshingly cool water. He swam with easy strokes to the far end of the pool, then as he grabbed hold of the coping, realised that Beth Travers was beside him. He could see her eyes now; they were green. 'That was a very nice dive,' she said.

'Thanks.'

'Clive was telling me . . .'

'I heard.'

'It's a shame, though.'

Shane shrugged. 'Life goes on.'

'I suffered a loss recently myself,' she said in a voice that was slightly husky.

'Oh?'

'My husband.' She sighed. 'It isn't easy.'

'I'm sorry.'

Beth smiled at him. 'Oh well, as it turned out, it was probably the best thing for both of us.' Then, as Shane looked at her blankly, she laughed. 'Don't look so serious. He's not dead. We're divorced.' She studied him intently for a moment. 'Would you like to have dinner with me tonight?'

The question was so unexpected that Shane almost swallowed a mouthful of chlorinated water. He spluttered. 'That would be great. Thanks.'

'It's a date then. I'll get you a towel.' She pulled herself up out of the pool. The water streamed from her tanned, slender body.

As she headed for the house to fetch a towel for Shane, Clive came to the edge of the pool and glared down at Shane in the water. 'Okay, you've had your fun. Now it's back to work.' He didn't look at all happy. Shane grinned up at him, then slid beneath the water.

They bickered all the way back to Ramsay Street that afternoon. Shane told Clive about Beth Travers' invitation to dinner, and that made it even worse. 'I can't help if she's got good taste,' Shane said shortly as they came in through the back door of the Ramsay house.

'Good taste, my foot,' Clive slammed the door behind him. 'I was just working up to ask her out myself.'

'*Working*?' Shane snorted. 'Who did all the working, pal?'

'Don't call me pal . . . pal.' Clive poked him savagely in the ribs.

'Hey, you can't fight on an empty stomach,' Max Ramsay said as they stomped into the kitchen. 'How about a beer?' He handed each of them a can from the refrigerator.

Shane opened his and took a hefty swig from it. He jerked his head towards Clive. 'He's dirty on me because I got a date with the boss,' he told his father.

Max began to goad Clive. He never needed much encouragement to goad Clive Gibbons from next door. 'That was a bit rough of you, mate,' he said to his son. 'Clive was looking forward to a nice time out there.'

Shane drank some more beer. 'You enjoyed yourself, didn't you, Clive?' He turned to his father. 'He sat on his backside all afternoon, trying to chat up Beth.'

'I was discussing plans with her,' Clive muttered defensively.

'Oh sure.' Shane winked at his father.

'And it's *Mrs* Travers to you,' Clive said pompously.

'I reckon you blokes will stay in business about five minutes the way you're going,' Max observed cheerfully.

Shane nodded to Clive. 'Yeah, well, he's going to have to start putting his back into it.'

'And *you're* going to have to stop flexing your muscles,' Clive retorted.

'That's what happens when you work, pal. You should try it some time.'

'You've got him there, son,' Max said proudly.

'He wouldn't even *have* a job if I didn't come with the ideas,' Clive growled.

Max grimaced. 'You mean, like the last little venture you had.'

Putting down his beer can, Clive began to back away. 'I don't have to put up with this.'

'Suits me,' Shane said with a grin. 'I've got to get ready to go out, anyway.'

Instead of having dinner at her house, Beth Travers suggested they might go out somewhere. There was a small Italian place she knew which was quite cosy, and the food was excellent. Shane said that was okay with him. They had pasta and drank red wine. They talked about different things. She asked Shane a great many questions about himself. It wasn't a late night.

'Bored, was she?' Clive sneered when Shane told him this in the morning.

'You're not jealous, are you?'

Shane was just finishing his breakfast when Clive arrived. 'I just hope we've still got a job to go to this morning,' Clive said irritably.

Shane drained his teacup. 'Why wouldn't we?'

'Well... who knows *what* you were up to.'

'I've already told you,' Shane was stung to retort. 'I got home quite early.' He looked up at Clive with narrowed eyes. 'Yes, you *are* jealous,' he decided.

Their voices had been raised. Shane's aunt, Madge, came into the kitchen. 'You two cut this out at once,' she said crisply. 'You can be heard up and down the street.'

'I'm sorry, Madge,' Clive said.

Shane was on his feet. 'He was the one who started it.'

'I tried to stop it,' Clive countered.

Shane looked from Clive to his aunt. 'I haven't done anything to be ashamed about.'

'Oh?' Clive's laugh lacked any vestige of humour. 'So it's normal to take a client out for half the night, is it?'

'Shane?' Madge's expression was grim. 'What have you been doing?'

'Not what *he* thinks, that's for sure.'

'It's the principle of the matter,' Clive said.

'I beat you to it.' Shane gestured impatiently. 'Some principle.'

Clive appealed to Madge. 'You talk some sense into him.'

'I would if I knew what both of you are arguing about.'

'Beth Travers,' Shane explained. 'The woman we're working for. She took me out for dinner last night.'

'You didn't go?' Madge was a woman who saw immorality lurking in every corner. 'Did you?'

'Yes, he did,' Clive supplied helpfully.

'Shane, how could you?' Madge was shocked. 'Haven't you got any sense at all?'

'It was absolutely harmless.' Shane was on the defensive.

'Nevertheless,' Madge said importantly, 'you should know better than to mix business with pleasure.'

'Or have any pleasure at all,' Clive contributed. 'At least not with Mrs Travers.'

Madge's eyes widened. 'She's married?'

'Divorced,' Shane told her.

'That doesn't make a scrap of difference.'

'Nothing happened.'

'It's the principle of the matter, Shane.'

Clive glanced at his wristwatch. 'We'd better get to work.'

Shane stood up. 'I can hardly wait,' he said sarcastically.

'That's no way to speak to Clive,' Madge admonished him. 'Without him you wouldn't have a job at all.'

Clive smirked. Shane was furious. They drove in silence to Beth Travers' house.

It was another hot day. Stripped down to his shorts, Shane attacked the ground with a shovel while Clive, on his hands and knees, set about pulling weeds. Suddenly, he yelped. Shane stopped digging.

'Now what's the matter?'

Holding his finger, Clive scrambled to his feet. 'I've cut my finger. On a piece of this sword grass here.'

'Give me a look.' Shane looked at the injured finger. There was only a little blood. 'That's nothing.'

'It'd be a different story if it was *your* finger.'

'You just don't know the meaning of work, do you?' Shane said shortly.

'Do you think I'm trying to get out of it?'

'I know you are.'

'Good morning.' Wearing only her brief swimsuit, Beth Travers was coming across the terrace towards them.

'Hi,' Shane greeted her with a grin.

'Morning,' Clive said, sucking the blood from his finger.

Beth was smiling at Shane. 'I did enjoy last night.'

'Me, too.'

'We must do it again some time.'

'Can't wait.'

'Neither can the garden,' Clive remarked drily.

'Well, I'll let you two get on with it then.' With that same insouciant swing of her hips, Beth sauntered across to the reclining chair beside the pool.

'I can't work with this finger,' Clive complained.

'You don't know how to work, full stop.'

'I'll take the shovel,' Clive said. 'You do the weeds.' Shane handed him the shovel. 'It's just as well I'm here to organise things.'

A few minutes later, as Shane was grappling with the weeds, his finger was pricked by a thorn. He yelped. 'Something wrong?' Clive asked with a concern that was patently false.

Shane had the finger in his mouth. 'Thorn in my finger.'

'Show me.' With his brow furrowed in mock concern, Clive examined Shane's finger. 'Oh, what a shame. Poor little pinky.'

Frowning, Beth hurried towards them. With a disapproving glance at Clive, she took Shane's finger. 'That looks quite nasty. 'I'll take it out for you.'

'If it's not too much trouble,' Shane said gratefully as Beth continued to hold his throbbing finger. Clive held up his own finger on which there was a glistening drop of blood.

'What about me?'

Beth was leading Shane away. She looked back at Clive. 'You'll just have to work on your own.'

Shane grinned at Clive whose expression at that moment was thunderous.

A short while later, he was lying back on the chair beside the pool, nursing his injured and now bandaged finger watching Clive at work with the shovel. Beth was inside the house fixing some lunch. She had told him to relax and not strain himself. She had been most solicitous.

After some moments, Clive threw down the shovel in exasperation. 'Are you coming back to work, or not?' he demanded. Shane held up his bandaged finger. 'Mine's worse than yours,' Clive muttered resentfully.

'Not according to the boss,' Shane said. 'Besides, you're lucky I don't sue you for workers' compensation.'

Beth came out of the house, carrying a tray of drinks and sandwiches. Clive rushed across to take the tray from her. 'Thank you,' she said, barely acknowledging him. She beamed down at Shane. 'Would you like a swim before lunch? I thought I'd have one.'

'Great idea,' Shane said, springing up from the chair.

They swam, splashed each other, and raced each other to the end of the pool, while Clive watched them sullenly from beneath the striped umbrella.

'You're pretty damned pleased with yourself, aren't you?' Clive said later, after they'd had lunch and Shane was breaking up the ground with the pickaxe. Clive was digging half-heartedly at the remaining weeds. Shane gave him a long-suffering look; he was quite fed-up with Clive's surliness. 'I put myself out to take you into the partnership, and then you go and do something like this to me.'

'Face it, Clive, old bean,' Shane said. 'You're just a bad loser.'

'Oh right,' Clive said, rolling his eyes heavenward. 'Any other character flaws you'd like to point out to me while you're at it?'

'I'm not really all that interested in you. Or her.'

'Is that a fact?' Clive said with a glimmer of hope. 'Then you'd better go and tell her that, hadn't you? Like right now.'

Shane was leaning on his pickaxe. 'Well, well, well. Look who's jealous.'

'Don't be ridiculous,' Clive snapped. 'I just don't think it's fair to Beth, that's all. I mean, look at her. She can hardly take her eyes off you.'

Which was quite true. Shane had been aware of her scrutiny from behind the dark glasses as he worked; it had made him a little self-conscious, a little uneasy. Perhaps Clive was right. It was only fair. 'I'll tell her,' he agreed.

Clive was still regarding him hopefully. 'When?'

'In my own good time,' Shane said irritably. He hefted the pickaxe. 'Now, how about we get some work done around here?'

In disgust, Clive picked up his shovel and began to hack ineffectually at the ground with it. Beside the pool, Beth Travers stretched luxuriously, then rising from the chair, dived into the pool. Clive yelped in pain as the shovel struck his foot.

When she came out of the pool, her wet body glistening in the sun, she called Shane across to her. Shane was sweating rather freely; he ran his forearm across his brow; the water in the pool looked very tempting.

'Why don't you stop working for a few minutes and talk to me?' she suggested.

Although he was strangely reluctant to do this, Shane didn't see how he could refuse.

Beth sat on the edge of the pool, her legs dangling in the water. 'You've earned a break,' she said. 'You're working twice as hard as your so-called partner.'

Shane sat down beside her. 'Clive's not really used to the work.'

'It shows.'

She edged a little closer to him. 'When do you think we can go out again?' she asked.

Shane felt awkward. 'You don't want to be spending *all* your time with the hired help, do you?'

'If I like a man, I like him.' She was watching him intently. Her feet kicked idly in the water. 'It doesn't matter *what* he does for a living. So . . .' She gave him an expectant smile. 'What about tonight?'

Shane glance across at Clive who was still working feebly away with the shovel. 'Ah . . . no, I can't.'

'Tomorrow then?'

He looked at her. Her body was slowly drying in the

sun. A small pool of water had formed on the coping beneath her. Shane decided that this was the moment to tell her what was on his mind. 'Look, Beth ... this is really awkward, but my going out with you has caused problems between me and Clive. He thinks it's unprofessional.'

Frowning in annoyance, Beth glanced at Clive. 'Tell him it's got nothing to do with him.'

'I can't do that.'

'All right then. I will.'

Swinging her legs up from the water, she stood up and began to head across the terrace towards Clive. Shane also jumped to his feet. 'Beth, I can't do it because I happen to agree with him.'

She stopped and turned back to face him. 'I see,' she said tightly.

Shane could see the disappointment in her eyes. 'No, you don't.' He gestured apologetically. 'Look, Beth, I think you're a terrific person – I really do – and I enjoyed our date. But you just can't go on mixing business with pleasure.'

'Is that the only reason?' Now there was a calculating look in her eyes. 'You'd go out with me again if you weren't working for me?'

Shane considered that for a moment. 'Yes, I would. Of course.'

She smiled at him then turned away. 'Clive,' she called. 'Could I see you for a moment.'

Clive came running. His expression was eager. 'Yes?'

Beth smiled at him sweetly. 'I just wanted to say, firstly, that you should learn to mind your own damned business, and secondly, that I've changed my mind. You're both fired.'

Clive's mouth fell open. Shane looked at her in astonishment. Beth was still smiling sweetly.

*

'I mean, what precisely did you say to her?' Clive demanded after they had returned to the Ramsay house and Shane had listened to him raving on for the past half hour or so with a long-suffering air.

'Only what you *wanted* me to say, mate.'

Clive was striding about the room, waving his arms in agitation. Shane sat impassively on the living room couch with his own arms folded. 'Great. Yeah;' said Clive. 'Blame it all on good old Clive.'

Shane took a deep breath. He was only just managing to keep his cool. 'Listen to me,' he said tautly. 'You haven't stopped bellyaching since we formed this so-called partnership. So we lost the job. So what? There'll be others.'

'"There'll be others", he says.' Clive clapped his hands to his head and performed a strange pirouette. He was being very dramatic. 'Just like that. Oh boy. And dozens of lovely, lonely ladies just like Beth Travers queuing up to have us do their gardens.'

'If she means that much to you,' Shane suggested, 'why don't you get yourself over there and ask her out?'

Clive glowered at him fiercely. 'You're nuts. You're bonkers. Why the hell would I want to go out with someone who's just given me the sack?'

Unable to grasp the logic of this, Shane looked up at the ceiling – but there was no elucidation to be had from that quarter. The kitchen door opened, and a moment later Max Ramsay came into the room. He stopped in surprise when he saw them. 'I thought you two would be lazing around the lady's pool, sipping champers,' he remarked.

'The lady's just given us the boot,' Shane told him morosely.

'Why?'

Shane shrugged. 'She didn't really have a reason.'

Clive snorted. 'I can give you one in two words –

Shane Ramsay.'

'Give it a rest,' Shane growled.

Max threw himself down into an armchair. 'The bosses have always had it in for the workers,' he said gloomily. 'Nothing's changed.'

'That's not true,' Clive protested. 'Some of them are scrupulously fair. Take me, for instance.'

Shane looked up at the ceiling again. 'Please,' he sighed.

'Some boss *you* turned out to be,' Max said testily to Clive. 'Got yourself fired along with your worker. Stroke of pure genius.'

Clive dropped into one of the other armchairs. He looked thoroughly dejected. Shane looked from his father to his partner. 'You know, sometimes I really wonder about the company I keep,' he observed.

Suddenly, Clive leapt to his feet again. His expression had cleared. He rubbed his hands together. He was brisk and businesslike again. 'What we need around here is some action.' He turned to Shane. 'Have you still got that list of contacts from the last time you were contract gardening?'

'I think so. Somewhere.'

'Then start searching, man. Got to drum up some business. Can't afford to let the grass grow under our feet.' He swung to face Max. 'This is going to be big, Max,' he cried enthusiastically. 'I can see Shane and I being millionaires before the decade's out.'

'With *you* calling the shots?' Max was staring at him in disbelief. 'Huh!'

Shane was out shopping when Beth came to the house to see him the following morning. When he returned, he found her waiting there with Max, who was obviously impressed with this woman who looked just as stunning fully clothed as she did when clad in only the briefest of bikinis. Shane was taken aback to see her.

'I came to offer you your job back,' she said after they had greeted each other. Max had offered to leave them alone, but she had waved him back to his seat; what she and Shane had to discuss wasn't necessarily private.

'But I don't understand,' Shane said. 'When you sacked us . . .'

'I don't want Clive back,' Beth said with a friendly smile. 'Just his partner.'

Shane shook his head. 'Thanks, Beth – but no thanks. Clive and I are a team.'

He carried the bag of groceries out into the kitchen. Beth followed him. 'Shane, for heaven's sake. Don't be so silly.'

He placed the groceries on the table. 'You might thinks it's silly, but we have an agreement.'

'Don't be a drongo,' Max said gruffly as Shane and Beth came back into the living room. 'The lady's offering you your job back. That gorilla's not interested, anyway.'

'How would you know?'

'Well, he's not exactly what you'd call a born gardener, is he?'

'We're partners, and a deal is a deal.' Shane was standing his ground. Beth was watching him with her lips slightly pursed. 'You understand that, don't you?'

'So, it's all or nothing.'

'I'm afraid so.'

Beth picked up her bag then stared at him evenly for a long moment. 'You drive a hard bargain, Shane, but all right. I'll take you both back.'

'Are you sure about that?' Shane was genuinely bewildered by this woman who changed her mind at the drop of a hat. 'I mean, you're not going to suddenly change your mind again when you get home?'

'You can have it in writing if you like.'

Shane grinned at her. 'Starting tomorrow?'

'First thing.'

'I'll take back what I said earlier about bosses,' Max told his son. 'You blokes seem to have found yourselves a good one.'

Beth laughed. 'And to celebrate the re-establishment of our working relationship,' she said to Shane, 'what do you say I take you out to dinner tonight?'

There it was again. Shane felt nicely trapped. He didn't know what to say. When he said nothing, Beth sighed and shook her head. 'Oh, Shane, you're not going to tell me that Clive has to come, too, are you?'

Shane smiled at her rather sheepishly, feeling quite foolish. Max laughed outright.

When he thought more about it, Shane began to have reservations. There was a price to pay for their restored fortunes – and he felt it in his bones that it wouldn't stop with the dinner that night. That was just the beginning. He felt he was becoming embroiled in something that, if he wasn't careful, would gather impetus so that before long he would find himself powerless to do anything about it.

The feeling of entrapment was kicked along drastically that afternoon when a courier arrived with a small parcel for him. Puzzled, he opened the parcel, then the box inside – and saw to his amazement that it contained a rather expensive wristwatch with a worked gold band. There was a card with it which read, 'To my favourite gardener. A small gift to remind you not to be late tonight.' It was signed, 'Beth'.

'She seems to have taken a shine to you,' Max observed as he examined the watch.

'I'm sending it back,' Shane said.

Clive was with them. He and Shane had been discussing woodchips when Beth's gift arrived. 'You're kidding.'

'It's getting out of hand, Clive.' The watch definitely had to go back. Beth had had no right to send it. Shane was quite annoyed with her.

'And we could be out of a job,' Clive pointed out. 'When someone gives you a present you don't slap them in the face. And you don't look a gift horse in the mouth.'

Max looked at his son. 'I must say the woman must be pretty hard up to send presents to someone who only shaves three times a week. Nip it in the bud, son,' he said seriously. 'You'd be making a big mistake if you don't.'

'He *can't* send it back,' Clive protested. 'Be cutting our throats if he does.'

'Then he's going to have to do something,' Max said grimly. 'Because he'll end up sorry if he doesn't.'

Shane was experiencing the suffocating sensation that the world was closing in around him. Yes, something did have to be done. The watch had to go back.

But she refused to take it back. She was most insistent. Tears came into her eyes. She told him how hurt she would be if he refused her little gift. She threatened to make a scene in the restaurant. Finally, Shane relented; he really didn't have much choice.

He had just returned home when the telephone rang. It was Beth to tell him that she missed him, that she was lonely in an empty house. It wasn't natural, Shane thought when he was finally allowed to hang up. It was getting out of control. He wished he had been more firm about the watch.

In the morning, Clive dropped Shane at the Travers' house. He wasn't staying; he had promised to give a number of quotes. 'When will you get back?' Shane asked as they unloaded the van.

'I mightn't be back.'

'What?'

'Those quotes could take time.'

Shane glanced nervously towards the house. He made

up his mind. Enough was enough. 'I'm not going to wear this.' He threw down the rake he was holding.

Clive picked up the rake and handed it back to him. 'We haven't got our money yet, lover-boy.'

As they came around the side of the house, Beth emerged from the back door with a cool drink in her hand. Shane experienced a sinking sensation. 'You made the running, kiddo,' Clive muttered out of the side of his mouth. 'You handle it.' He dropped the tools he was carrying and hurried back up the path. Feeling quite unhappy about being left alone with the woman, Shane steeled himself to face her.

She offered him the drink she was carrying. He said, no thanks, not now, there was work to be done. 'There's plenty of time,' she said. 'I want to talk about last night.'

Shane didn't want to talk about last night – he didn't want to talk about anything. Beth's presence was making him uneasy. 'Well... actually... there *isn't* plenty of time. We start a new job shortly.'

She looked at him in surprise. 'You won't be coming back?'

'I have to work somewhere else,' Shane said lamely.

'You won't be coming back,' Beth said in a tone of finality.

'Beth...'

'It's all right.' She turned away. 'It had to happen sooner or later.'

Shane stared after her as she walked back to the house. He felt even more uncomfortable now that he had told her he wasn't coming back.

He worked furiously that morning. The sooner the job was finished, the sooner he could get away. At lunch time, Beth came out of the house with a plate of sandwiches and something to drink. 'You didn't have to do that,' Shane chided her. 'I brought my own lunch.'

'I like to do it.' She put the plate down on the table.

'For you.'

Shane looked at her unhappily. She was making it very difficult for him. 'You hardly know me.'

'I know what I need to know.' She smiled at him. 'It's the eyes. You have such nice eyes.' She gestured towards the plate of sandwiches, but Shane didn't really have much of an appetite at that moment. 'Last night . . .'

'I'm not such great company,' Shane broke in. 'Maybe you should get out more often.'

'I don't care where I am,' she said quietly as she watched him with an intense and discomfiting expression. 'I care more about who I'm with.'

'Well . . . things don't last forever, you know.'

She placed her hand on his bare chest. His heated flesh tingled at the contact. 'You tan so well. But you should be careful not to overdo it.'

Gently, Shane eased her hand away. 'Beth . . . look, I've got to finish the job. And I think we should both face the facts. Don't you?'

'I have.' She was smiling at him lazily. 'But facts are not enough, Shane. It's the future that matters for us.'

As she moved away, Shane watched her with a worried frown. What had she meant? He wished he knew.

When Clive turned up again that afternoon, Shane complained to him about Beth Travers. 'You really have to do something about her.'

'I'd love to,' Clive said with a wink. 'But she fancies you.'

'She's practically blackmailing me into spending time with her.'

'You could always scream rape,' Clive said facetiously.

'And you could get her off my back,' Shane retorted. 'If you don't I'll quit.'

Clive regarded him sombrely. 'You mean it, don't you?'

'I'm not putting up with it,' Shane said with a nod.

Clive gave him a reassuring pat on the shoulder. 'Leave it to me,' he said. 'I'll sort this out.'

Beth was lying beside the pool. Shane watched as Clive spoke to her for some minutes before she suddenly sprang to her feet and hurried into the house. Rubbing his hands together and looking highly pleased with himself, Clive returned to Shane's side. 'All taken care of, mate. Problem solved.'

'How? What did you say to her?'

'Don't worry about it. She won't hassle you any more.'

'Clive, tell me what you said to her.'

'Easy,' Clive said cheerfully. 'I told her you're getting married next week.'

'What?' Shane stared at him in horror.

'You wanted her off your back, didn't you?' Clive queried innocently.

'Not that way,' Shane exclaimed. 'Everyone knows I'm not getting married.'

'She doesn't,' Clive told him. 'She took it without a murmur.'

'Didn't she want to know who I'm supposed to be marrying?'

'I told her it was Daphne.' Now Clive was looking a little shamefaced.

'Daphne.' Shane stared at him in shock. Daphne Lawrence. Well, at one time they might have had something going between them . . . but *marriage*? It was too ludicrous. 'How could you *do* that?'

'You asked me to help – remember?'

'But I didn't think you'd do anything as stupid as that,' Shane wailed. 'And what if Daphne finds out?'

'Look, she doesn't have to know,' Clive answered. 'And if she *does* find out about it somehow, I'll explain it.' He gave Shane another reassuring pat on the shoulder. He exuded confidence. 'Don't worry. I'll fix it for you.'

'You already have,' Shane said woefully. He had fixed it good and proper – and now Shane felt he was in a worse mess than before.

Clive had told Beth an out and out lie. As he worked, Shane worried about it. Finally, he threw down his shovel. 'I'm stopping. I've had enough.'

Clive was pruning a hedge. 'What's up?'

'I can't work any more today. I'm going.'

'Hang on. What about collecting our pay?'

'I'm not doing that.'

'Why not?'

'How can I face up to Beth now?' Shane said. 'She must think I'm a real creep after what you told her.'

'All right,' Clive said. 'I'll get it.'

Shane gathered up his pickaxe and shovel. 'I'll see you at home.'

'Hang on. How am I supposed to get back?'

Shane was only just managing to keep himself in check. 'Okay then. I'll load the van and wait for you. Just keep her away from me, that's all,' he added forcefully as he walked across the terrace to the path that led up the side of the house to the street.

'Typical Clive,' Max Ramsay snorted when Shane told him what had happened. 'That's just the sort of stupid idea he *would* come up with.' He eyed his son who was prowling restlessly around the room. 'What are you going to do about it?'

'I tried to get him to go back and tell her it wasn't true – and of course he wouldn't,' Shane replied in disgust. 'So I guess I'll have to do it myself.'

Max was dabbing at a paint spot on his overalls with a rag soaked in turpentine. 'I'd do it straight away if I were you.'

'The trouble is, she might start making a play for me again.'

'It's a hard life, son,' Max said with a chuckle.

'Can't you think of *some* way I can fix it?'

Max shrugged. 'I bet Daphne won't be so thrilled when she hears about it.'

That was an understatement. She would be furious. 'That idiot Clive...'

'He's your partner, son,' Max said in gentle admonishment.

That evening, having built up sufficient resolve, Shane tried to call Beth, but there was no reply. 'It'll keep till morning,' Max remarked.

'No, it won't.' Impatiently, Shane replaced the receiver. 'I've made up my mind. I want to set things straight with her.'

'If she's not in,' Max calmly pointed out, 'she's not in.'

'I think I'll go out for a drive. Can I borrow your van?'

'The keys are in my overalls. In the laundry, I think.'

'Thanks.'

When he came back into the living room with the keys, Shane was taken aback to see Beth Travers talking to his father. He hadn't heard the doorbell. 'Beth!' he exclaimed. 'What on earth are you doing here?'

Beth was looking very subdued. She nodded to a parcel wrapped in brightly coloured paper which was standing on the table. 'I brought you a wedding present. But now your father tells me there's no wedding. That it was just a story. I feel such a fool.'

'Sorry, son,' Max said, rising to his feet. 'But you *were* going to tell her.' He left the room. Shane stared helplessly at Beth.

'I can explain...'

'I should go,' she said a little shakily.

'No, please. Stay for a few minutes. I want to explain.'

'You don't need to. I understand.'

'You don't understand.'

'Shane, I feel stupid, embarrassed. Please let me go.'

She moved towards the door. Shane reached out and took hold of her arm.

'I feel bad, too. I didn't want to hurt you.'

'You lied to me.'

'I didn't. It was Clive who made up that story.'

'You let me go on believing it.'

'I'm sorry.'

'I'm sorry, too,' Beth said quietly. Her lower lip quivered. 'I shouldn't have harassed you. I hope it all works out for you.'

Shane released her arm, then crossing to the table, picked up the parcel she had brought. 'You'd better take this.'

'No,' she said with a sad shake of her head. 'You keep it. You'll find a use for it one of these days.'

There was still the job to finish at the Travers house. There was the landscaping to be completed, and a retaining wall to be built. They didn't see so much of Beth who tended, for the following few days at least, to remain inside the house. This might have had something to do with the weather which, while still warm, was overcast. On a couple of days it rained. Then one day the sun was back again, and Beth decided to find fault with the retaining wall Shane and Clive had put up the day before.

'It's out of alignment,' she said.

Clive was unmoved. 'Not according to my spirit level.'

'Well, it looks out of alignment to me. And I'm the one who has to live with it.' She fixed him with a cold stare. 'Fix it, will you.'

'I'll have to go to the hardware shop for more cement,' Clive told her grudgingly.

'Then I suggest you do that.'

The reclining chair was back out beside the pool. Beth settled herself on it. Clive fished out his keys from his bag. Shane was alarmed. 'You promised you wouldn't leave me alone with her.'

'Haven't got much choice, have I, mate?' Clive returned. 'I'll only be gone ten minutes.'

He was gone before Shane could protest further. Keeping a wary eye on the woman lying beside the pool, Shane began to shovel sand into a wheelbarrow.

Much to Shane's relief, Clive kept to his word and was back before long. They worked on into the afternoon. Clive was laying paving bricks which Shane brought across to him in the wheelbarrow. 'Starting to look like something,' Shane said approvingly, standing back to admire their handiwork.

'Out of chaos comes order,' Clive observed.

'No doubt Bathsheba over there will have some complaint to make,' Shane said wrily.

'She's the paying customer,' Clive reminded him. 'She's got a right to say if she doesn't like it.'

'Yeah,' Shane said doubtfully.

Clive glanced at his wristwatch. 'Oh hell,' he groaned. 'I promised to see this mate of mine.' Straightening, he brushed his hands briskly together. 'You could start breaking up the old pathway if you like.'

'No way.' Shane was horrified at the thought of being left alone with Beth again. 'I'm not sticking around here on my own.'

'Come on, mate.' Clive made an appeal to reason. 'How would it look if we both walked out? We're supposed to be trying to build up a reputation for reliability.'

Shane could see that he had a point. 'Yeah, all right,' he conceded, although not very happily.

'Besides, I don't think you'll have any trouble,' Clive said, picking up his bag.

Perhaps there wouldn't be any trouble, Shane thought. Beth had left him alone while Clive was picking up the cement, and there was no reason why she wouldn't leave him alone now.

'Where's Clive going?' Beth had just come out of the house carrying two cool drinks on a tray.

'Some personal business,' Shane told her.

'Oh . . .' She seemed a little disappointed. 'I brought you something to drink.

'Not while I'm working,' Shane said rather stiffly.

'Come on, don't be silly,' Beth said with a smile. 'It's only a soft drink.' She appraised his glistening torso. 'And it *is* a hot day.'

Shane relented. He took one of the glasses which had cubes of ice bobbing around in it. 'Thanks.'

'Actually, I was hoping for a chance to talk to you alone.'

'Oh?' Shane was suddenly on his guard.

'There's no reason why we can't be friends, is there?'

'I don't know,' Shane said thoughtfully. 'I mean, it might be better if we kept a strictly business arrangement.' Beth turned around and walked into the house. 'Damn,' said Shane.

About an hour later, as he was setting up the boxing for some concrete, he looked up to see Beth coming down the path carrying a carton that looked quite heavy. 'Here, let me give you a hand with that,' he said, hurrying across to her.

'I can manage,' she said coolly.

The carton contained bottles of wine. 'Hey, come on,' Shane urged, reaching out for the carton. 'That's what I'm here for.' He grinned at her. 'That was our agreement, wasn't it? That Clive and I do all the heavy lifting?'

She didn't resist when he took the carton from her. 'All right then,' she said slowly. 'Yes, why not? It goes in the cellar.'

The cellar door was just beyond the back steps. Beth

opened it for him. Shane had to duck his head as he entered the cellar which was dark and cool inside. After the glare outside, it was a moment or two before his eyes became accustomed to the gloom. Along one wall he could make out shelves crowded with wine bottles.

'Quite a stock you've got here,' he was saying when, suddenly, the door slammed shut behind him, blocking off what little light had filtered in from outside. Startled, he put down the carton and turned back to the door. 'Beth.' He pounded on the door. He tried the handle but the door was locked. 'Beth,' he shouted more loudly. 'Come on. A joke's a joke . . . Beth!' He banged on the door more fiercely. 'Come on, Beth.'

But there was no response from the other side of the door. He listened, but could hear nothing. He couldn't believe this was happening to him. It had to be a mistake; or a joke of some sort. 'Beth, the door's jammed or something.' He gave a weak laugh. If it was a joke . . . 'Beth . . . are you there?'

Then she was speaking to him from the other side of the door. 'I'm not letting you out, Shane,' she said very seriously, dispelling any notion Shane might have had that it was just a joke. 'I mean it. You've got to stay there.'

'Come off it, Beth,' Shane cried. 'A joke's a joke. Let me out of here.'

'If I can't have you, then no one else can.'

Stunned, Shane could hear her footsteps as she ran back along the path. 'Beth?' But this time there was no response. Shane began to pound the door again. 'Hey!'

She wasn't going to let him out – that much was obvious to him. Just as it was obvious that she had meant every word she had said. The woman was demented. Shane lowered himself to the ground where he sat with his back against the wall. Clive would be back soon. He didn't know what Beth would tell him – but he would be bound to wonder where he was. Perhaps he would notice that the tools were where Shane had left them – unless, of course, Beth had taken the trouble to remove them.

He must have been sitting there for at least an hour, gloomily pondering his situation, when he was alerted by a sound. He looked up to see a widening strip of light coming from the door, which, he saw now, was slowly opening. He leapt to his feet as Beth's figure appeared around the door.

'About time,' he cried out in relief. 'I want out of here.'

'No. Stay there. Get back.' With one hand grasping the door handle, she held up a key in the other. She looked nervous, but determined. 'It's a deadlock,' she told him. 'All I have to do is slam it, and you'll be here all night.'

Shane moved more warily towards her. 'Beth, this isn't funny.'

Beth backed further into the opening. 'I'm not letting you out.'

Shane could see that she meant it. A more subtle approach was required. He stopped. 'All right, all right. You want me to stay here – is that it?' Beth nodded. Shane continued to tread carefully. 'You want to talk?' Beth nodded again. 'Okay,' Shane said, 'but wouldn't we be more comfortable in the house?'

'I'm not stupid, Shane. You'd be gone in five minutes.'

Too right he would. 'You know, Beth, I think this is against the law.'

'Who cares?'

'I do,' Shane told her. 'I want to get out of here.' It was just too ludicrous; he still couldn't really take the situation seriously. 'I mean, what do you think you'll achieve? You can't just keep me locked up. Clive will be here soon to pick me up.'

Beth shook her head. 'He's been and gone.'

Shane gaped at her. 'What?'

'Ten minutes ago. I told him you'd left.'

'He'll be back,' Shane said uncertainly.

'Not for at least two weeks. I told him I'm taking a holiday.' Now Shane really *was* beginning to worry. The woman was definitely around the bend; there was no telling what she would do next. 'You've *got* to be joking, Beth. This is crazy.'

She was watching him intently. 'You mean, *I'm* crazy, don't you?'

That was more or less it. 'Of course not,' he said quickly. 'It's just...' he raised his hands... 'a crazy thing to do. I mean, what do you *want* from me? What am I supposed to do? Stay here forever? What good would that do either of us?'

'I thought, if I could get you here, away from everyone else... I thought we could...' She sighed. 'I don't know.' She was struggling to explain herself. Shane could see she was close to tears. She was holding the key loosely in her hand. 'I should have known it wouldn't work,' Beth said helplessly.

'Come on, Beth.' Shane's tone was soothing, persuasive. 'Just tell me what you want. We can work it out. I'm not going to hurt you.' He was edging closer to her as he spoke.

She saw what he was doing. She became angry. 'Don't try and con me Shane,' she cried. 'I'm not as stupid as you think.'

Abruptly, she ducked out through the opening, slamming the door behind her. In his rage, Shane kicked at the door.

There was no other way out of the cellar; Shane had checked it thoroughly. He studied the labels on the wine bottles in the shelves. He was thoroughly fed up.

'Shane, are you there?'

Very funny, Shane thought. 'I'm here.'

'I brought you something to eat.'

'Very considerate.'

'Sandwiches.'

'All I want is to get out of here, Beth. So open the door.'

'I wouldn't have had to lock you in if you would have just listened to me.'

There was no point in upsetting her; she sounded agitated enough as it was. 'All right, all right, I'm sorry. It's just getting on my nerves, being stuck down here.'

'I know.'

She knew? 'So?'

Shane's mind was working. If he could get her to open the door . . . He could take her by surprise, grab the key . . . but he had to be careful not to alarm her first. 'You said something about food,' he said. 'I'm starving.'

'Sandwiches. Roast beef with horseradish, avocado and salad.'

'Great,' Shane called enthusiastically. 'We can have a picnic.' He glanced up at the shelves of wine. 'I hope you've brought a corkscrew.'

'A what?'

'Never mind. Just bring in the sandwiches.'

Moving soundlessly across to the door, he flattened himself against the wall beside it. 'Wait a minute.' From outside, Beth's voice was suspicious. 'Where are you?'

'What do you mean, where am I? In this rotten cellar – where else?'

'You *do* think I'm stupid, don't you?'

'Now, look . . .'

'I want you over by the far wall,' she commanded. 'Then call out so that I can tell that you're not waiting just inside the door to grab me.'

Shane moved away from the wall. After he had taken a few steps, he placed his hand over his mouth to give a muffling effect to his voice. 'Okay.'

'Are you right by the wall?'

Shane was creeping stealthily back towards the door. 'Uh-huh.'

'Stay there.'

There was the sound of the key turning in the lock, then, slowly, the door began to open, letting in a wedge of daylight. Shane readied himself for the attack. The door opened wider. Carrying a tray, Beth made a tentative appearance. Shane threw himself forward. Beth screamed when she saw him coming at her, and dropping the tray, tried to back out through the doorway. But Shane was too quick for her. Grabbing her arm, he hauled her into the cellar and held her in a tight bear hug. She began to struggle. She was the prisoner now.

'You wanted to talk? Okay then, let's talk.' She was crying out. She tried to bite him. 'Come on, calm down,' Shane ordered. 'That's enough. I'm not hurting you.'

Beth was livid. 'You cheat,' she cried. 'You liar. It was just like you to trick me like that.'

'I had to do something.' She sank her teeth in his shoulder. 'Ow!' he yelped and as he involuntarily released her, she darted across to the door and slammed it shut. She turned back to face him with a triumphant gleam in her eyes.

'There. Now we're both stuck in here.' She held out both hands, palms uppermost. 'See? No key. I left it outside.'

Desperately, Shane tried to open the door, but it was locked again. He rounded furiously on the woman who had brought him to this predicament. 'Clever. Really clever, Beth. Well, you've got what you want now, haven't you? The two of us alone together. Romantic, isn't it?'

Beth stooped to pick the plastic-wrapped sandwiches from the floor. She handed one of the packs to Shane.

They sat in the cellar, their backs against the wall. Beth watched Shane as he gloomily munched a sandwich. She herself wasn't eating. 'You see, Shane, I had to do it. It might seem incomprehensible to you, but it was the only way. You were always putting me off, telling me some lie or other just to get rid of me.' She was becoming upset again. Shane was feeling uncomfortable. Perhaps she did have a point at that. 'Are you enjoying your sandwich?' she asked quietly.

'Yes. Tasty.' It was one of the roast beef ones.

'It tastes all right to you?'

'Fine?'

'I mean . . . not funny, or anything like that?'

What the hell was she on about now? 'What do you mean – funny?'

She was still watching him steadily. 'I don't know. Bitter perhaps?

'Why should . . . ?' Shane had the sandwich halfway to his mouth. His hand froze as he was struck by an awful possibility. He stared at Beth who was smiling at him rather strangely. 'What have you done?' he croaked. He waved the half-eaten sandwich at her. 'What have you put in here?'

Beth continued to watch him. Shane threw the sandwich away. He sprang to his feet. Cold sweat beaded his forehead. He was suddenly very frightened. He had already eaten half the sandwich – and if she *had* put anything in it . . . It was possible. Anything was possible. Who knew how far a woman like this would go? Demented, crazy, a loony . . . 'I just wanted you to know what it feels like to be scared,' she said softly.

He glared at her. 'You mean . . . ?'

'Have another sandwich. They're quite all right.'

But Shane had suddenly lost his appetite. He sat glumly against the wall and wondered how they were going to get out of there. 'I didn't really plan it,' Beth said after a while. 'It was just one of those things you suddenly find yourself doing.'

'Really?' Rising to his feet, Shane took down one of the wine bottles from the shelf. There was no corkscrew, but Beth had brought a paring knife for the fruit she had included on the tray. He picked up the knife from the floor and began to dig the cork out of the bottle with it.

'You were treating me as if I had the plague,' Beth said bitterly. 'I couldn't get near you. And all I wanted to do was talk.'

'Now's your chance. We've got all the time in the world.'

'You don't know what it's like to be lonely, do you?' Her eyes were wide and dark in the dim light as she looked up at him.

Shane prised at the cork with the knife. 'Of course I do.'

'Not really.' She shook her head. 'You've got your family and all your friends.'

Shane glanced down at her. 'Haven't you?'

'Oh sure.' Her voice was suddenly brittle. 'All I have to do when I'm in trouble is reach out, and there they are.' She waved her arm at the rows of wine bottles.

Shane finally managed to work the cork free from the bottle. He scooped up the two plastic cups Beth had brought down to the cellar with her, and filled them both with red wine. He handed one of them to Beth. 'Perhaps if you found a job . . .'

'With my qualifications?' She gave him a small, sad smile. 'I was married as soon as I left school. I was only seventeen at the time.'

Shane remembered. She had told him that on their first night out together. 'There must be *something* you want to do . . .' He sipped his wine.

'Sure. Find a man who really loves me, have some kids, be happy.'

100

'And until then?'

There was a long pause. Shane drank some more wine then looked at her enquiringly. He sensed her reluctance. 'Nothing,' she said finally. 'It's stupid.'

'What?' Shane persisted.

'Well,' she said shyly. 'I did think once that I'd like to be an architect.' She picked up a sandwich and began to eat it.

'This wouldn't have happened if you had been straight with me from the beginning, Shane. All I wanted was a friend.'

'You mean, if I'd treated you like a mate instead of a woman, we wouldn't be here now?' Shane eyed her sceptically.

'I would have settled for that.'

'Well, I'm glad *that's* been cleared up.' He sighed. 'Now what do we do?'

But instead of answering him, Beth began to unbutton her blouse. Shane looked at her in dismay. Surely not . . . She couldn't expect . . . It was hardly the time or the place. Seeing his expression, Beth smiled, then slipped her hand quickly inside the blouse. She brought out her hand. In it, she was holding the key. Laughing, she handed it to him. 'We open the door,' she replied.

Shane shook his head at the strangeness of it all, then took the key she was holding out to him, and grinned at her. 'At last,' he said in huge relief.

Five

When her adopted daughter breezed in from New York, Helen Daniels was determined that her visit should go smoothly, that there shouldn't be any tensions – but at the same time she knew it wouldn't be easy. For one thing, Rosemary was successful; she was doing very well for herself in America. Then there was Paul's attitude towards her. Paul still held a grudge – and in fact, Rosemary arrived in the middle of the argument between Helen and her grandson, neither of whom realised until it was too late that she had quietly entered the house and had overheard much of what they were saying about her.

Helen had been fussing about, getting things ready for the dinner she fervently hoped would be a success. 'I don't know why you're making such a fuss,' Paul observed sullenly.

Helen was irritated by his attitude. 'She's my daughter, and I haven't seen her for two years.'

'She's aggressive,' Paul muttered. 'She's pushy.'

'Paul!' his father exclaimed.

'Well, it's true.'

Helen's irritation was passing into anger. 'I will not allow you to spoil Rosemary's homecoming.'

'That's right,' Jim Robinson said. 'This is a family reunion. Everyone is to give Rosemary a warm welcome.'

Paul stood up. 'You can all stop worrying. I won't be

here for dinner.' He glared at the others. 'And while she's here, you won't be seeing much of me at all.'

'Good,' Helen snapped. 'If that's how you feel, then stay out as much as you like.'

'I will. I just can't stand know-all women.'

'Paul!' Jim was also on his feet. 'I won't have this from you.'

'What have you got against her?' Scott asked his brother.

'She fired me – remember?' Paul replied tightly. 'That holiday job I had before I started Uni. She got me the job, then sacked me – just to throw her weight around.'

'That's not the way it happened,' Helen said shortly.

'That's exactly the way it happened,' Paul retorted.

Jim was glowering at his son. 'Paul, you'll apologise to your grandmother.'

Paul stood his ground. 'What for? Telling the truth?'

'You're behaving like a spoilt child.' Helen could have struck him at that moment for his intransigence.

'Now listen,' Jim growled. 'Just stop this.'

'Don't stop on my account,' Rosemary said quite pleasantly from the doorway.

'Rosemary!' Helen exclaimed as everyone turned towards the newcomer.

Rosemary smiled around the room. 'I've always said, there's no place like home,' she remarked as she smiled around the room.

Rosemary had always been an ambitious girl, while Helen's other daughter, Anne, was more of a home-maker, like herself. But then Rosemary wasn't her natural daughter; other genes had set to work in her. She had gone on to great things. The Rosemary Daniels Corporation, as she told them at dinner that night, was involved in management consultancy and investment packaging, with marketing and publicity divisions.

103

Mainly, it dealt with company purchase and takeovers – and now she hoped to set up an Australian division. But that depended on her finding someone suitably qualified to run it. She couldn't be away from New York for too long.

'Business must be booming,' Jim observed.

'Actually, it is,' Rosemary said thoughtfully. 'I must try not to be too proud of myself, but things are going well.'

'Then, *be* proud.' Helen beamed warmly at her adopted daughter who was making such a success of her life. '*I'm* proud of you.'

After the others had gone to bed, Helen had time to be alone with Rosemary. There was much to talk about. Helen asked her if there was a special man in her life. Yes, there was, Rosemary said with a fond smile. He was very special. He was an artist. His name was Gerard Singer. Helen had heard of him. 'But I don't know how permanent it will be,' Rosemary said wistfully.

'But you love him, don't you?'

'Yes, and he loves me. It's just that . . . well, things have gone wrong before.'

'You're still not concerned over that business with Brian, are you?' Helen asked solicitously.

'I still think about Brian,' Rosemary said quietly. She sighed. 'It was probably for the best that we did split up. But it hurt. It still hurts. And I've never forgiven Paul for his part in it.'

'Is that right?' Paul queried sharply from the kitchen doorway. Shocked, both women swung to face him. Neither of them had heard him come in.

'Paul,' Rosemary breathed.

Paul's face was flushed. He stared angrily at Rosemary. 'You're deluding yourself. Everyone in the firm knew the truth.'

'What truth? What are you talking about?'

'Brian was only having a fling with you,' Paul said tautly. 'When you became too serious he had to find a way to get rid of you. And that's the truth, whether you like it or not.'

Rosemary was obviously shaken. 'Paul, you're wrong.'

'It's the reason I had to leave.'

They faced each other across the kitchen. 'It's not,' Rosemary shot back at him. 'You just weren't suited for that job. Be honest, Paul. I didn't need to make up excuses to fire you She pointed an accusing finger at him. 'And you haven't changed. You still won't take responsibility for your failure.'

Paul looked away from her. 'It wasn't just me. That whole place was going downhill.'

'Yes, thanks to Brian,' Rosemary said shortly. 'He was hardly more competent than you. I could have saved that business if he had given me free rein with it.'

'It doesn't change anything,' Paul muttered. 'He still had you sack me just to cause a rift with you.'

Rosemary's smile was scornful. 'If you believe that, I can only pity you.' She picked up her bag. 'Now I'm going back to my hotel.'

As Helen walked with her to the door, she glanced fiercely back over her shoulder at her grandson who was doing everything he could to spoil what should have been a happy occasion. 'Wait here, Paul,' she ordered. 'I have some things to say to you.'

'I'll be back in the morning,' Rosemary said at the front door.

'Promise?' Helen was holding her hand.

'I'll sleep off my jet lag, then call in as soon as I feel alive.'

They held each other for a moment in a close embrace, then Helen watched her as she walked down the path to her hired car. She waited until the car had driven away before turning back inside to confront her grandson. She

105

launched straight into the attack.

'How dare you speak to Rosemary like that,' she cried. 'Barely off the plane after two years away, my daughter, your aunt, a guest in this house – and you behave like a malicious child.'

Paul was backing away as she advanced relentlessly on him. 'But she's only your . . .'

'Yes, she *is* adopted,' Helen savagely interrupted. 'I adopted her, and I love her, and I will not allow you to spoil her visit. This is my house as much as yours, and you will respect that, Paul. I will not let you drive my daughter away.'

The following day, Rosemary dropped her bombshell. She led up to it by talking about time and space and Grand Central Station, of which Helen's house put her in mind, what with people coming and going all the time. Then there were all the things Helen had to do – the cooking, the washing and ironing, cleaning. 'I couldn't imagine having a workload like yours,' Rosemary said, sipping her coffee.

'But I do have some spare time for my painting,' Helen pointed out with a laugh. 'And I happen to enjoy mothering and grandmothering, most of the time.'

Rosemary regarded her seriously. 'Don't take me too lightly, Mum,' she said. 'I mean, how much time do you *really* get to paint? Truthfully now.'

Helen considered for a moment. 'Five or six hours a week,' she said.

Rosemary raised her eyebrows. She looked very cool, very elegant in the kitchen of the Robinson home. Her voice bore just the slightest trace of an American accent. 'Only five or six? In a whole week? You probably spend three times as much as that cooking meals for a family who are quite capable of doing it themselves.'

'I don't believe my family take advantage of me,' Helen said, a little peevishly.

106

'No, but they certainly take you for granted.'

'I don't think so,' Helen said.

'At least you could have some time and space of your own, a chance to find yourself.'

'I'm very happy, Rosemary.' There was an edge to Helen's voice.

'Mum.' Rosemary was watching her intently from across the table where they were sitting over morning coffee. 'I'm going to ask you to do something for me.'

'Well, yes, of course.'

Rosemary hesitated; suddenly she seemed to have lost some of her poise. 'What if it was something that meant your leaving this house?' she asked finally. 'Leaving this family?'

Helen was shocked. She stared at her adopted daughter. 'What do you mean?'

'I've been thinking, Mum. About the Australian end of my consultancy. I need someone I can trust.'

'More than that, I would say,' Helen said. 'Surely you'll need a person who is already experienced in the field, and who knows exactly what to do.'

Rosemary frowned slightly. 'A lot of people experienced in this game are vultures. If I pick out someone who is concerned only about what's in it for them, my business and profits could go down the drain. That's why I need someone I can rely on. You, for instance.'

It had come straight out of the blue; Helen was totally unprepared for it. She poured some more coffee for Rosemary. 'But I don't know the first thing about company takeovers or cash injections, or whatever else it is you do.'

But Rosemary refused to be put off by such details. 'All you need is tact and common sense,' she told Helen. 'Once you've handled one deal, the others will all follow the same pattern. Believe me, I've worked to a set of guidelines in all my dealings in the States. Australia will be no different. All you have to do is take it one step at a time.'

She was making it sound so easy. 'And if I did take you up on your offer,' Helen said thoughtfully, 'why would I have to leave the family?'

'I'll have to be truthful, Mum.' Rosemary put down her cup. 'It's a rat race. The work will be demanding and time-consuming. The hours will be long. You simply won't have time for anything else. But the rewards – that's something else again. Travel, an excellent salary . . .'

'I don't know,' Helen demurred. 'I don't think I could just walk out on my family for a job. I've always admired your business sense, Rosemary, so I know you wouldn't ask me if you didn't think I could handle it. But . . .' she smiled apologetically . . . 'I still don't feel confident about my ability.'

'You'd have plenty of time to learn,' Rosemary persisted. 'All I ask at the moment is that you think about it.'

The more she thought about it, the more Helen had to confess that the idea did have certain attractions. In fact, she was quite tempted by it.

But when she told Jim about Rosemary's offer, he was incredulous. Helen became quite infuriated by his attitude. 'Come on, Helen,' he laughed. 'I can hardly see *you* as a wheeler and dealer. Anyway, she needs someone with a good knowledge of the financial world.'

'That isn't what she said. It's more important for her to have a level-headed person she can trust.'

'Fair enough,' Jim said. 'You fit the bill as far as that goes. But is it enough? I mean, what would you know about things like corporate structure. It would take you years to learn.'

Helen thought he was being just a little patronising. 'Rosemary isn't worried about that. She's quite happy to ease me into the position over a period of time. Frankly, Jim,' she went on, 'if I do decide to take her up on her offer – and I am tempted – I'd like your blessing.'

'Why would you need *my* blessing?' he countered.

'It would mean leaving you and the children.'

'Is that what she told you?' he asked resentfully.

'It wouldn't be fair to Rosemary if I didn't put all my efforts into the business. I would be away a lot, for a start.'

'I still can't understand why she would offer the job to you.'

Helen was stung. 'Perhaps *she* feels I could do it,' she said coldly.

Jim gestured placatingly. 'I didn't mean to be rude. I'm only trying to be practical. You've never had any experience of the business world. I'm worried that you might end up over your head.'

'Thank you for your concern,' Helen said drily, 'but I'm quite capable of making my own choice about what's best for me. I don't need your help for that.'

Helen was washing the breakfast dishes when Rosemary arrived early the next morning. Helen was preoccupied; she still hadn't made up her mind about Rosemary's offer. When he had learned about the possibility of her leaving them, Scott had been upset. He had begged her to stay for what were obviously selfish reasons. Paul had been non-committal. There was also little Lucy to consider, but she was staying with some friends in the country, so at least Helen didn't have to contend with her appeals for the moment. Not that it would be any easier when the time came for her to return home.

'I might have guessed I would find her at the sink,' Rosemary remarked sourly to Jim who was sitting at the table, reading the morning newspaper.

Jim rustled his paper in annoyance. 'For your

information, the family prepared their own breakfast this morning,' he briskly informed her.

And made such a mess of the kitchen, Helen thought grimly. Of course, she had been the one to clean it up.

'Big deal,' Rosemary said with a snort of disgust.

Her attitude made Jim bristle. 'Now listen here, Rosemary,' he said gruffly. 'I'm willing to admit that Helen does most of the housework. But by the same token she's well aware of the fact that we appreciate it.'

'And what reward does she get for that?' Rosemary's expression was set as she looked down at him, then across at Helen who had just finished the dishes and was untying her apron. 'Chapped hands?'

Jim lifted his shoulders a fraction. 'Look, Rosemary,' he continued, 'Helen's a home-maker, but that's a very special occupation in my books, and it certainly runs rings around your offer.'

'Rubbish,' Rosemary exclaimed. 'No woman in her right mind would give up the chance of a stimulating career just for the sake of cleaning someone else's bathroom.'

Helen stood beside the sink with her arms folded, looking from one of them to the other, quietly absorbing what they were saying. 'That's the only way you can equate Helen's worth, isn't it?' Jim challenged. 'Well, I'll tell you something about that, Rosemary. To my kids, she's more than just a grandmother; she's their friend, and I can understand it if they don't want her to go.'

'For all the selfish reasons,' Rosemary returned snappishly. 'That's the way kids are.' Helen was beginning to feel a tightness in her throat. The kids would miss her terribly. She would miss them. 'She won't stop being their friend simply because she chooses to live a life of her own.'

Jim flung his paper onto the floor. 'Since you've

arrived here, you've done nothing but try to undermine Helen's position in this house, and as far as I'm concerned...'

'Stop it!' Helen cried. She had heard enough; it was just going on and on, this terrible bickering. 'I can't stand it any more. I've made up my mind.' There were tears in her eyes. Both of them stared at her in astonishment. 'I'm staying here. With Jim. With the kids. I'm not going anywhere.'

Jim looked relieved. Rosemary's expression was grim. 'You can't do this to yourself.'

But Helen was certain. 'I'm sorry.'

Jim stood up, and crossing to her, took her hand. 'Helen, we're grateful. But I don't want you doing this because you're sorry for us.'

It wasn't that... 'Of course that's why she's doing it,' Rosemary said sharply, 'as you are well aware. So spare us the hearts and flowers.'

Jim flared up at her. 'It's nothing to do with hearts and flowers.'

'Stop it!' Helen shrieked. 'Just stop this. Please.' They stared at her in shocked silence. 'I need this family,' she told them in a calmer tone. 'I'm used to them.' It was as simple as that.

Rosemary was clearly put out. 'If that's your decision,' she said in a strained voice, 'so be it. I'll just have to live with it.'

Yes, Helen thought after she had gone. They would all have to live with it. She was absolutely positive she had done the right thing.

If Rosemary had departed in a huff as a result of Helen's rejection, Helen knew she was not the sort of person to carry a grudge for long. All the same, it was with a great sense of relief that Helen let her into the house again that evening.

111

'I just couldn't leave things like that,' Rosemary explained. 'But I *was* disappointed. I had tailored this job especially to you because...' she gave Helen a small, rueful smile; her gesture was one of regret... 'well, I'm family, too.' Helen held her arms out to her and they embraced. Helen knew everything would be all right. 'They're Anne's family, too,' Rosemary said, moving away from Helen, 'and I love them. But they've had a big, big share of you. And now the children are older...' She gestured again.

Momentarily saddened by the mention of the children's mother who had died so tragically young, Helen said with a smile, 'So much for my business acumen, a broad experience...'

'Knowledge of people is the heart of any business,' Rosemary told her. 'The rest you could have learned.' She shrugged quite eloquently. 'However, as you've chosen otherwise...'

Yes, Helen thought, there was no point in discussing the matter any further; her mind was quite made up. The door opened, and Paul entered the room, looking rather pleased with himself. 'Another day in the insurance jungle,' he greeted Helen as he put down his briefcase. 'Just signed up a big superannuation scheme.' He saw Rosemary and his smile faltered. 'Hello, Rosemary.'

Rosemary, too, was making an effort. 'It seems congratulations are in order.'

'Thanks a lot.'

'Super is certainly where the future is,' Rosemary observed. 'As a matter of fact, I still have some contacts from my insurance days. I'll pass on a couple of names, if you like.'

'I'd appreciate that,' Paul said pleasantly, picking up his briefcase. 'Now, if you'll excuse me. First the sale, then the paperwork.'

Helen was pleased that they were both making the

effort. The two of them really could get on together, she felt, if they tried. She had a sudden idea.

'Paul's very good at his job,' she said, after he left the room. 'He would be a very good manager – much better than I would have been. You know, Rosemary,' she said eagerly, 'it's worth considering.'

Rosemary looked doubtful. 'I don't know . . .'

'In fact, he would be ideal.' The more she thought about it, the more certain Helen was. 'If you thought *I* could run the business for you, then there's no doubt that Paul could do it.'

'I still don't know,' Rosemary said with a frown. 'It's a matter of staying power, for a start. Apart from that, he just doesn't seem to be mature enough.'

Helen overrode her reservations. 'I think you might be pre-judging him. He has matured a great deal. If you'd only take the trouble to talk to him, I think you'd be surprised.'

'Well . . .' She considered briefly . . . 'if it will make you happy, I'll talk to him.'

'Oh, good.'

'But I wouldn't hold out much hope.'

'We'll see.' Helen was feeling quite confident that it would work out all right.

Rosemary was watching her curiously. 'Why are you so keen for me to employ him, anyway?'   'It's a great opportunity,' Helen replied with a shrug. 'And he *is* family. I think that counts for something.'

'Did it count with you?'

Helen smiled at her. 'Of course it did,' she said. 'It always has. You should know that.'

Six

The writing was on the wall. His days were numbered. Max Ramsay was preparing to meet his Maker. He had become quite philosophical about the prospect.

It was Danny and his mate at the bank who had brought home the realisation that mortality was upon him. He had been in the pink of health before then, and now... It was those bloody racehorses. He could have been a millionaire by now. Every time he thought about it, he experienced another pang.

It was Danny, the economic genius, who told him that he should have backed the horse each way, instead of just to win. If he had done that, he would have three chances to get his money back. He could show his father how to do it properly. He could compute the odds and there would be very little risk. Such a whizzkid, he was. Max should have known that it would turn out to be a disaster.

He had just won five hundred bucks on a horse called Nifty Lad, which had come in at twenty-five to one. He had been ecstatic. He had even hugged Madge. He had put twenty dollars on the horse.

'Listen, Dad, seriously,' Danny said. 'I know how you can do much better than today, and more often. If you're interested, I could work it out on the bank's computer. A mate of mine on the computer course has shown me how to make it work.'

It was over Max's head. It all sounded American. 'I'm not into this electronic wizardry,' he said.

'It's *not* magic, Dad,' Danny protested zealously. 'It's logic. You feed in things like past form over twenty races, weight carried, the class of race – you know – maiden, intermediate, open, how good the jockey was – and then you project it forward to form. One kilo equals a length and a half at the finish, and so on.'

It was still well over Max's head, but he was impressed nevertheless. 'Can you *do* all this stuff?'

'Just watch me.'

'I'm not putting any money on it,' Max said firmly.

'No, but we can do it as an exercise at first. If it works, the money will come later.'

Max couldn't see that there was anything wrong with that. 'All right,' he said. 'I suppose you've got to be in it to win it.'

When he learned that Danny's mate from the computer course had won every race in the metropolitan area that same Saturday, Max didn't believe it at first, but Danny insisted it was true. It had been a clean sweep. 'I'm not kidding you, Dad. It's easy. You'll see when we get our system going.'

'Did he put any money on them?' Max asked.

'No,' Danny replied. 'He only does it as an exercise.'

'More fool him,' Max said with a grimace. 'Is your system the same as his?'

'He showed me how to do it.'

'Well, then...' Maybe it wouldn't do any harm at that. 'A few small bets then,' he said. 'Just in case.'

But Danny didn't think they were quite ready for that yet. 'It would be better if we just started in theory,' he objected. 'Until I get the programme worked out properly.'

The more he thought about the possibilities, the more impatient Max became. 'But look what we missed out on Saturday. Think what we could have won if we'd backed all his winners.' He shook his head. His mind was made up. 'No, Danny. I think we might have to risk a little cash.'

Danny was set to work in the bank computer. He came up with seven horses, but wasn't sure on which of them he should place Max's money. Max told him the lot – split it up, he said. And to Max's amazement, they all came in. He had checked his winnings at the local betting shop. Almost seven grand. It was a miracle. He deferred to science. When Danny came home from work, Max hugged him. 'Every one of them, boy. Every single one.' He hugged Danny again. 'You'll do me, son. No more small time, eh? No more business or property worries.' Danny was looking rather subdued. Max was making plans. 'The thing to do is plough the whole lot back in,' he chuckled.

'But, Dad . . .'

'Build it up some more.' He placed his arm proudly around Danny's shoulder. His son, the expert, the money-maker, the architect of Max's fortune, the cornerstone of which had already been laid. Mansions and yachts and corporate piracy . . . Visions shimmered before him. 'We're riding a fortune, Danny. Riches untold.'

'Dad, I didn't back the horses.'

'That's okay, son.' Max was only a little disappointed. 'Fair enough, you're entitled to use your discretion. If you felt a couple of the nags weren't up to it, I accept your judgement.'

'But I didn't back *any* of the horses, Dad,' Danny cried unhappily. 'Not a single one. I got cold feet. I didn't lay out a cent.'

Max's arm dropped from his son's shoulder. A joke – that's what it had to be. 'That's very funny, Danny,' he said with a forced smile. 'That's very droll.'

'It's true, Dad.' Danny was looking utterly miserable. 'I'm sorry, but it is.' Max's smile vanished; he could see

116

now that the boy was telling the truth. 'I know you told me to go ahead, and everything – but I thought you'd got a bit carried away, you see. I mean, it was a hell of a lot of money. I'm very sorry.'

'Sorry?' Max gaped at him as his fortune crumbled into dust. 'Sorry?' He turned to Madge who so far had been silent. 'Did you hear that? He's lost me thousands of dollars and he's sorry.' He shook his head in bewilderment. 'I don't believe it.'

'What else am I supposed to say?' Danny muttered defensively.

Only a moment before, Max had been full of goodwill and bonhomie; now he was full of rage and self-pity. 'I'll never forgive you for this,' he shouted, brandishing a clenched fist. 'Never!'

'Max, calm down, for heaven's sake.'

Max hardly heard Madge. Why him? What had *he* ever done to anybody that he should be treated like this? He paid his taxes, taking no more shortcuts than the next man. He had always been fair. 'For once in my life I thought luck was on my side,' he wailed as he prowled around the room. 'For once – just once – I thought I was going to make an easy quid. God knows I deserve it. But no. Oh no.' Danny flinched as his father, wildly gesticulating, rounded on him. 'This idiot here has to screw it all up.'

'Stop being dramatic, Max.' Madge's voice was like a whiplash. 'You should be proud of Danny; he obviously has a very sensible attitude towards money.'

That was her, that was his sister. Max glared at her. No wonder her husband had cleared out; no wonder the worm had finally turned. 'You keep out of this, Madge.' He wheeled back to his traitorous offspring. 'You amaze me – do you know that?' he bellowed. 'You're not even capable of following a simple little instruction.' He vigorously tapped his temple with a forefinger. 'Some-

117

times I wonder if there's not something wrong with you.'

Danny found his voice. 'But what if I *had* placed the bets, and the horses had lost? Then you'd be yelling at me for that.'

'But they didn't lose, did they?'

'It's the last time I listen to Des, that's for sure,' Danny said.

'Des?' Max's eyes widened. Des Clarke? 'What does *he* have to do with it?'

'It doesn't matter,' Danny murmured uncomfortably.

'No, come on.' Once again, Max was advancing threateningly on his son. 'Out with it. What does Des Clarke have to do with this?'

'I talked it over with him,' Danny answered with obvious reluctance. 'He was the one who thought it would be better if we played safe.'

'Oh, did he now?' Max stormed towards the back door. 'I see. Just because he's a bloomin' bank manager he thinks he knows better than me.' He wrenched open the door. 'Well, we shall see about that.'

Des Clarke lived two doors further up the street, on the other side of the Robinsons. He was home. Max didn't bother with the formalities. 'Well? What have you got to say for yourself?' he demanded.

'Is something the matter?'

'The matter?' Max snorted furiously. 'He asks me if there's something the matter?' He jabbed Des's chest with his finger. 'I understand you gave Danny a bit of advice this morning.'

Standing in the doorway with the lighted hall behind him, Des puzzled over this for a moment. 'You mean, about throwing your money away on the horses?' he queried at last.

'It was a ticket to paradise,' Max told him shortly. 'Except that you decided to interfere. You stuck in your opinion when none was called for – and every one of those seven horses won.'

'You're kidding?' Des was staring at him in amazement.

'No, Des, I am not kidding.' He prodded Des's chest again with his finger. 'And I'm holding you and Danny responsible. Six thousand eight hundred and forty-one dollars – that's what you cost me. I shall expect a cheque by the end of the week.'

To take his mind off his worries, Max spent the next few hours down at the local pub where he drank quite a number of beers, met a few mates and won a darts match. By the time he arrived home, a little unsteady on his feet, he was feeling quite sentimental. He was no longer angry. He was whistling tunelessly as he let himself in through the back door.

Danny was still up, seated at the kitchen table. He looked up guiltily as his father came into the room and closed the book that was open on the table in front of him. Max beamed at him with affection. 'Hello, son.'

'Hi.' Danny was sitting stiffly at the kitchen table. 'Have a good time?'

'I most certainly did.' Max was weaving from side to side on his feet. 'I won a darts match and had a damn good talk with my mates.' He pulled out a chair and sat down next to Danny. 'And do you know what we talked about? Children, that's what. Kids, like you. And I discovered something.' He leaned confidentially towards his son. 'You're not such a bad lad after all.'

'Oh,' Danny said without enthusiasm. 'Good.'

'Hey, you wouldn't like to make your poor old Dad a cup of tea, would you?'

'All right.' Danny stood up, and crossed the room to switch on the jug.

'What's this, son?' Max peered at the books on the

table in front of him. 'Homework?'

'Sort of,' Danny said tensely.

'But you don't go to school any more.' Picking up one of the books, Max studied it. Mathematics. He saw Scott Robinson's name on the cover. He swelled with pride. 'It's Scott's. You're helping him with his maths.' He spoke with emotion. 'I'm proud of you, Danny, sitting here, late at night, working away . . . and why? Because you want to help your mate. That's what life's all about, you know.'

'Is it?'

With some difficulty, Max's eyes focussed on Danny, that selfless, hard-working and totally misjudged son of his. ''*We're* mates, aren't we?'

'Sure.'

'I was a bit rough on you before.'

'That's okay, Dad,' Danny said uneasily.

'Just beacuse you didn't place that silly old bet.'

Hope flared in Danny's eyes. 'Well, Dad, like you say, we're mates. Perhaps you can forgive and forget, eh?'

'Of course I can,' Max said emphatically, while Danny's expression showed relief. 'I still expect you to pay me back, of course, but I don't hold it against you.'

Danny's face fell. 'Gee, thanks, Dad.'

'That's all right, son.' Max waved expansively. 'That's quite all right. Any time.' He continued to beam at his son.

In the morning, Max's temper was foul. He cursed the birds which had awoken him. He cursed everyone. His head was throbbing. He glared at Danny. He picked at his breakfast.

There was a way of getting that money back – and that was by the same means it had been lost, or not won. Max instructed Danny to get to work on that computer of his and draw up a list of certainties.

Max called into the bank just after it had opened for

business that morning. 'Have you got that list yet?' he asked, crossing to the counter where Danny and Des Clarke had their heads together over a computer print-out.

Danny looked up glumly. 'Um... not exactly.'

'What do you mean – not exactly?'

'It's raining at the track,' Des supplied.

'Just a minor adjustment,' Danny said.

'Right.' Max nodded affably. 'Can't be too careful, eh?' He turned away from the counter. 'I'll come back in an hour or so.'

But when he returned, the list still wasn't complete. Danny gave him the names of the first three horses. Max left and placed his bets. As he had expected, they came in easily. Max was jubilant. 'We're going to make a killing,' he told Des on his return to the bank.

'I think that's what is worrying Danny,' Des said wrily.

'Eh?' Max looked at him hard.

'Doesn't matter.'

Danny joined them with another print-out. 'Have you got the rest of them?' Max demanded.

'Yeah.' Danny began to read from the sheet while Max jotted the names on the back of a withdrawal slip. 'Oriole Lady... Spartacus... Smooth as Silk... Crispin's Choice...'

Max looked up sharply. 'What do you mean – Crispin's Choice? I backed her once. Five horses in the race, and she came in sixth.'

Danny was unmoved. 'The computer says she's due to improve.'

Well, if that was what the computer said... Max wrote Crispin's Choice. 'No system's foolproof, you know, Max,' Des said worriedly. 'Maybe you should quit while you're ahead.'

Danny lent his own weight to the suggestion. 'Des is

right. There's no such thing as a certainty. All the computer can do is pick the most likely winner. Things could still go wrong.'

Max wouldn't hear of it. He had the greatest faith in modern technology. 'No way,' he said. 'You boys are onto a great discovery. It just takes a bloke with the nerve to carry it through – and that's where I come in.' He glanced down at the last name he had written. 'Crispin's Choice, eh? Well, well, well.' He winked at Danny and Des who didn't seem to be sharing his own enthusiasm. 'We'll make a packet.'

They all came in, one after the other, without fail – just as Max had known they would. He was beside himself with excitement. What an afternoon it was. 'Here's to us,' he cried, raising a can of beer to Shane and Clive Gibbons who had just arrived back from work. Max had already had quite a number of beers. 'I reckon I'll be able to retire soon. A professional punter – that's what I'll be then. All you need is a good system. You've got to be scientific. Use your noggin...' He tapped his own noggin... 'Like me. Started off with five hundred bucks and look at me now.' He was becoming more and more excited. 'Can't lose. Made a packet. Crispin's Choice – you beauty! Won by a length and a half in the last race.'

'Take it easy, Dad,' Shane urged him. 'You'll blow a fuse.'

Max laughed, and laughed. He was on the verge of hysteria. 'Ah... Dad?' Danny's voice cut through the jollity. Max looked across the room to where Danny, his very own boy, was standing in the doorway with Des Clarke. Max grinned and spread his arms. 'There's my boy,' he hooted. 'Good on you, Danny. Have a beer.'

'Just a minute, Max.' Des Clarke was moving towards him. Max wondered why he was looking so serious. Danny, too, for that matter. It was a time for celebration. No room for gloom. Reaching into the refrigerator, Max began to hand out the beer cans.

'How much have we made so far? Are we into the six figures yet?'

'Not exactly,' Des replied solemnly. 'No.'

'Max chuckled gleefully. 'But still very healthy, eh? That last race – I nearly bust myself when he romped in. Good old Crispin's Choice. Who would have thought it? I hope you put the lot on him.'

'We put the lot on all right,' Danny said woefully, 'but . . .'

'You beauty boys.' In his exuberance, Max hugged Danny, then punched Des playfully on the shoulder. 'We've done it again.' Holding his beer can aloft, he began to waltz around the room.

'Max, please . . .' Des was following him. 'Just listen a moment.'

Max placed his hand on Des's shoulder. 'Des, my boy, whatever you want, you've got it. You need money? A loan? It's yours. Anything you want.'

'We put the money on the wrong horse,' Danny blurted out.

It took a moment for it to register with Max who was just then thinking about the sauna he was considering having installed in the back yard. Then, when it did register, his mouth fell open. 'Huh?'

Des explained. 'The guy on the computer made a mistake when he came up with Crispin's Choice. He corrected it, and got Drover's Dream.'

'We couldn't get hold of you,' Danny said. 'We tried . . .'

'You put all the money on Drover's Dream?' Max asked in a voice that was strangely hollow.

'Yes,' Des replied.

Max was thunderstruck. 'It came in last.'

'We know,' Danny said miserably.

As the awful realisation of what had happened began

to sink in, Max was aware of a strange buzzing in his ears. The faces in front of him sprang into sharp focus then receded until they were quite blurred. 'You . . . you lost all my money?'

'Sorry, Dad.'

'You . . . you *morons*!' Max roared. 'You drongos. All my money. You threw it away . . .'

'Dad, calm down.'

'It's not worth getting upset about,' Clive Gibbons said.

'I'm *not* upset,' Max yelled in anguish. 'I'm . . .'

Suddenly, as the pain lanced across his chest, Max gasped, and clutching his chest, his eyes bulging, his face purpling, he groaned and sank onto a chair. His breath was coming with great difficulty.

'Come on, Dad,' Shane said with a nervous laugh. 'You're overdoing it a bit, aren't you?'

Max's eyes were staring wildly. He was still clutching his chest. Clive Gibbons was bending over him. 'He's not fooling, Shane. It could be a heart attack.' He looked up from Max. 'Call an ambulance. Come on, move it,' he rapped when Shane hesitated. As Shane ran to the telephone, Clive checked Max's pulse. 'Danny, Des, help me lay him on the floor,' he ordered.

'Shouldn't we be giving him the kiss of life, or something?' Des queried.

'Don't be stupid,' Clive retorted. 'You can see he's still breathing. Just help me get him on the floor.'

As they began to move him, Max recognised Clive's face only inches from his own. 'Leave me alone.' He was still finding it hard to breathe. 'What do you think you're doing?'

'Dad.' Danny's voice was a little shaky. 'Are you okay?'

'Just take it easy, Mr Ramsay,' Clive urged Max. 'Shane is calling an ambulance.'

'Ambulance?' The pain in Max's chest was abating, but he still felt weak. 'Who needs an ambulance?'

'You do.'

'No, I don't. Just had a bit of a turn, that's all.'

'I hope that's *all* it was,' Clive said seriously. 'But it could have been your heart.'

Max didn't like the sound of that at all. He was worried, but he wasn't about to admit it. 'You can cancel that ambulance,' he said as Shane came back into the room. 'I'm not going off to any hospital.' He noticed Shane's quick, worried glance at Clive. 'I don't care what *he* says. I won't be going in any ambulance, so you may as well go and save them the trouble.'

With a shrug, Shane turned back to the telephone. 'Then at least go to your doctor,' Clive advised Max. 'Let him check you out.'

'And be laughed out of the surgery?' Max rejoined. 'It was just indigestion – not surprising after eating one of Madge's pies, then having these two clowns walk in to tell me I've just lost a fortune because of their stupidity.'

'It's also stupid to take risks,' Clive said. 'If it's just indigestion, that's good. You can take some medication for that. But you should at least make sure.'

Max didn't want to make sure. If they told him that there *was* something wrong with him ... No, best not to know. Live on in blithe uncertainty. No news was good news. He fixed Clive with a baleful glare. 'What would *you* know about it, anyway?' he challenged.

'Enough to know that you shouldn't take chances with your health,' Clive told him. 'I'm a doctor.'

'You?' Max couldn't believe it. Neither, it seemed, could anyone else in the room, judging by the audible gasp that greeted this statement. 'A doctor?' A man who once made his living in a gorilla's costume?

'I do know what I'm talking about,' Clive said quietly. 'I could check you out myself, if you like.'

Max was appalled by the thought. 'You're not touching me,' he said fiercely. A doctor? This clown? It was quite impossible. Or was it? With all the strange things that had been going on lately, Max had to concede it might have been possible at that.

'I don't understand how anyone can be so pigheaded about their own health,' Clive said sorrowfully.

'Pigheaded?' Max exclaimed. 'Great bedside manner you've got, haven't you?' He smiled ferociously. 'Come on, admit it. You were just trying to scare me. You're no doctor.'

'It's true.'

'There doesn't seem to be any point in my hanging around here,' Des said, edging away. 'I'll pop in later and see how you are. Unless you want me to drive you to the hospital.'

Max gave a strangled cry. 'If anyone mentions that word again . . .' He eyed Des narrowly. 'Yeah, you can do something for me. You can work out how to get my money back.'

'Yes, well, you'd better talk to Danny about that.'

Belligerently, Max turned back to Clive. 'Well, what are you waiting for? For me to drop dead.'

'For you to see sense,' Clive said. 'That's what I'm hoping, anyway. It's not unusual for people to be reluctant to see their doctor because they're afraid of the diagnosis.'

'Afraid?' Max glowered at this so-called doctor. 'I can take bad news as well as the next man, but I'm not going to be panicked by some unqualified chicken doctor.' He chuckled; he thought that was rather funny. A chicken doctor . . . 'Anyway, if you're a doctor, what are you doing in Ramsay Street, running a gardening business?'

'I wanted to see something of the real world,' Clive told him.

'What? Running around dressed up as a gorilla?

Playing the part of a chicken? What sort of a real world is that?'

'There's no harm in just having a check-up, Dad,' Danny said.

'No.' It was a question on which Max was totally adamant. There would be no check-up – and that, to put it simply, was that.

They were still trying to convince him to change his mind when the door burst open and Madge rushed in with a look of great concern. 'Oh no,' Max groaned. 'Who sent for you?'

'I've just heard.' Madge was breathless. 'Des said it was a heart attack.'

Max didn't know how much more of this he could take. They were all in some sort of cloud cuckoo land. 'I have *not* had a heart attack,' he yelled.

'Calm down, Dad.' Shane placed his hand on Max's shoulder.

'I don't know for sure it was a heart attack, Mrs Mitchell,' Clive said to Madge, 'but the symptoms were such that it could have been a warning.'

Madge regarded him closely. 'Des said that you're a doctor.'

'Yes, I am,' Clive said tersely.

'We haven't seen any proof yet,' Max said suspiciously.

Madge was still looking dubious. 'I don't understand that part of it at all,' she said, 'but all that matters now is what I should be doing to look after Max.'

Oh Gawd, Max thought in dismay; how much more of this could he take? 'Nothing,' he muttered.

'Stop being so stubborn,' Shane said in annoyance. 'At least, get yourself checked up.'

'No.'

'Think of us for a change, Dad. What are Danny and I supposed to do if you suddenly drop dead?'

127

Oh marvellous, bloody marvellous. Max was becoming excited again. 'That's nice, isn't it? Charming. Only worrying about yourselves.' He pointed dramatically to himself. 'How do you think *I'm* going to feel?'

'Shane, you're not exactly helping things,' Clive said sternly.

'What's the procedure now?' Madge asked Clive. 'A special diet, I suppose?'

'Diet!' Max exclaimed. 'That's a laugh. I was eating one of your pies just before it happened.'

Madge rounded on him savagely. 'How dare you, Max Ramsay. There's nothing wrong with my pies.'

Danny stepped in to keep the peace. 'Stop fighting,' he cried. 'Dad's sick, and all you can do is yell at each other.'

Madge was immediately contrite. 'I'm sorry, Danny,' she said. 'You're quite right.'

'What a fuss about nothing.' Max frowned up at Clive. 'What are you hanging around for?'

'Just keeping an eye on you.'

Danny returned from the bookcase with a medical encyclopaedia. 'We can look up heart attacks in here, Dad,' he said, seeking the appropriate entry in the book.

'Home diagnosis isn't a good idea,' Clive said.

That did it. If *he* didn't think it was a good idea, then Max thought it was a bloody marvellous idea. He reached for the book. Danny handed it to him. Max found the entry dealing with heart attacks. 'This will shut you up.' He began to read. 'The first signs of heart attack are shortness of breath...' he faltered... 'chest pains...' He slammed the book shut, his confidence shaken. 'Anyway, what would a book know?' he declared defiantly.

It was part of his defiance that he should go into the kitchen for a beer. He took the medical encyclopaedia with him. Taking a swig of the beer, he read some more of the chapter dealing with heart attacks. It didn't look good; it was very discouraging. Placing the beer can on the table, he felt for his pulse, but couldn't find it. That, too, was very worrying. He was about to take another swig of the beer when there was a slight twinge in the chest. That did it. He looked at the can in his hand, decided it wouldn't do him any good, then poured its contents down the sink.

Madge prepared him something special for dinner. Max looked at it with supreme distaste. 'What's this muck?'

'Steamed fish with sesame sauce, pureed spinach and carrots julienne.'

'It looks like soup.' Max pushed the plate away. 'What's it all coming to,' he complained, 'when a man can't even settle down to a good feed of steak and chips?'

'Please, Max,' Madge insisted. 'You may even like it, despite yourself.'

Max sighed. 'All right then. Give us some tomato sauce. Maybe I can save it.'

'Sorry.' Madge shook her head. 'No commercial products for you from now on. They're full of salt and sugar.' She picked up the beer can without which no dinner could even be considered, and tipped the beer down the sink before Max had a chance to do anything about it.

'Hey!'

'Eat up, Dad,' Danny urged, indicating the plate in front of Max. 'Preventive medicine is much better than a by-pass operation.'

'That con artist next door is behind all this,' Max grumbled, picking at his food.

Madge threw the empty beer can into the bin. 'You don't have to be a doctor to know that you should be watching your diet.'

'He's turning you against me,' Max wailed.

'Eat your dinner, Max.'

'Think of it as an investment in your future,' Danny said.

Angrily, Max pushed the plate towards him. 'Then *you* eat it. You're the one who needs a future.' Jumping to his feet, he headed for the door.

'Max! Where are you going?'

'To get myself some decent tucker. A hamburger – with the lot.'

In the morning, lying on the sofa with pillows propped around him, Max braved the medical encyclopaedia again. There was a hand mirror and thermometer on the small table beside him. He read aloud. 'The state of the whole patient reflects on the state of the heart. Particular attention must be paid to the pulse and blood pressure. The latter can be regulated in times of stress by deep breathing.' He breathed deeply, then felt again for his pulse. After some fumbling, he managed to find it. It felt fairly uneven to him. Looking around, he saw the hand mirror on the table beside him. He reached for it and immediately experienced a wave of dizziness. 'Oh God,' he groaned. He brought the mirror up to his face and peered closely at himself in it. He pulled down the lower lid of his right eye. It looked pink. He told himself he had anaemia. He slumped back on the pillows.

Madge came in from the kitchen. 'Do you want your breakfast?'

Max felt very weak; his life's force was ebbing away from him. 'I'm not very hungry.'

'You're not *really* going on a diet, are you?' Danny had just come into the room.

'It's all that junk food you ate last night,' Madge said disapprovingly. 'What time did you get in?'

'I don't remember. I'm too dizzy.'

Madge and Danny exchanged a worried glance. Shane

breezed into the room, then stopped when he saw how serious everyone was looking. 'What's up?'

'Dad's laid up again,' Danny told him.

'There's nothing wrong with me,' Max said weakly.

Shane studied him for a moment. 'You look a bit pale,' he observed.

'Maybe you'd better take the day off work,' Madge suggested.

'No.' Max struggled up into a sitting position. 'I can't afford it.'

'Don't worry, Dad,' Shane offered. 'I can take over.'

'I'm not dead yet,' Max growled. Bringing himself abruptly up onto his feet, he was assailed by another wave of dizziness. He dropped down again onto the sofa. Madge was immediately by his side.

'Are you feeling faint again?' She placed her hand on his head, and tried to push it down. 'Here . . . Put your head between your legs.'

Max ducked out from beneath her hand. The dizziness had passed just as quickly as it had come. 'Leave me alone.'

'It's basic plumbing,' Madge said in concern. '*You* should appreciate that. If the pipes are blocked, gravity sometimes helps.' She backed away before the ferocity of his glare. 'I was only trying to get some blood to your head.'

'If you don't stop acting like I've already got one foot in the grave,' Max growled, 'I'll blow a gasket.'

'Dad, I could use a job right now,' Shane said eagerly. 'You'd be doing me a favour. I could do all the heavy work.'

Ah . . . Max looked at his son. It was possible, after all, that there might be advantages to be had in not being well.

'One day off won't hurt,' Danny said. 'What have you got to lose?'

'Yes,' Madge concurred. 'You can spend the day lying down. I'll bring you digitalis tea every three hours.'

'Didi . . . what?' Max brusquely waved her away. 'All I need is a bit of peace and quiet.' He turned back to his older son.

'All right, Shane, you can help me out at work.' He glanced down at the medical encyclopaedia beside him. 'But I should keep on the move, or the body degenerates.'

'Work's not exercise,' Madge informed him.

Danny picked up the encyclopaedia. 'If he doesn't work, he'll worry,' he said. 'It says here . . .'

'Danny's right,' Madge broke in emphatically. 'You don't *need* extra stress, Max. I'll make a special lunch for you and bring it out to the site.'

Max was beginning to bask in the warmth of their concern – but he was also a frightened man. 'I think we should call Clive over,' Danny said, and Max's face clouded.

'Are you trying to kill me?' He could feel his blood pressure shooting up alarmingly. He took several deep breaths. 'All I need is a bit of support,' he said stoically. 'And I've got that right here.' He smiled wanly up at their concerned faces. 'With my family.' Obviously touched, Madge took his hand.

'No worries, Dad,' Shane said gently. 'You can count on us.'

Max's eyes filled with tears. He squeezed Madge's hand. He would miss them.

Convinced that he was on his last legs, Max drew up his last will and testament. He decided to give Shane his Vietnam medals.

'Gee, Dad,' Shane said, admiring the medals. 'That's a great honour. They'll be something to remember you by when you're gone.'

'That's why I'm giving them to you, son,' Max said

132

bravely.

Danny was given the old photograph album. There it was, a sentimental record of the family in pictures. There were photographs of Danny as a baby. 'But why are you giving it to me now?' Danny wanted to know.

'Just so there's no mistake about who has it after I'm gone,' Max told him solemnly.

Danny looked shocked. 'After you've gone?'

'Son, I may not have all that long to live.' Max was laying it on the line; grim reality had to be faced. 'I hope I *have* got more time, but just in case, I want to know my family won't fall apart after the event. I don't want any arguing over my possessions, so I'm giving them all away now.'

Danny's eyes were glistening; he was clearly very moved. 'But, Dad ... I don't *want* you to die.'

'It's not up to us, is it?' Max glanced up at the ceiling. 'What's Shane getting?'

'I've given him my Vietnam medals.'

Danny's mood changed abruptly. 'Your medals? But you always said *I* was going to get them. You *know* I wanted them.'

Max sighed wearily. The bickering had already started.

The pangs were coming more frequently now. Time was running out. More than ever now, Madge and the boys were pestering him to see a doctor. They employed every argument they could find. They wheedled; they were not above using moral blackmail. 'If you won't do it for yourself, Dad,' Shane said, 'you can at least do it for us.'

'I might,' Max said, more to get them off his back, then gasped as the pain struck him again.

But there was no getting away from it. Like it or not, he did have to see someone about what was happening to

133

him. There was no postponing it any longer. Reluctantly, he visited the local doctor without telling anyone he was going.

The examination was thorough. The doctor made notes, wiped his glasses and looked thoughtful. Max was braced for the worst.

'I think you know I don't believe in pulling punches,' the doctor said at last.

This was it. It was coming – the awful confirmation of what Max had known all along. 'If I haven't got long,' he said in a small, quavering voice, 'I'd rather know.' He would take it like a man. He would smile bravely, and perhaps toss off a little quip or two. Dr Carter would smile sympathetically, clasp him firmly by the shoulder, look him straight in the eye, and say something like, that's the way, Max, I knew you had it in you; you've got the stuff it takes. He would be full of admiration.

Dr Carter glanced at his notes. He pursed his lips then looked up at Max over the top of his spectacles. Max calmly awaited the sentence. No blindfold for him; he would wave it contemptuously away. The doctor spoke.

'Well, you are overweight, and from what you've told me, your diet is an invitation to heart disease. You drink far too much, and you do little or no exercise.'

'So what are we talking about, Doctor? Months? A year?'

'Well, I should hope a lifetime,' the doctor said. 'But if you keep up your present lifestyle, it could be considerably less. Fortunately, we do have a simple cure for chronic indigestion.'

'Indigestion?' Max gaped at him.

The doctor nodded. 'Indigestion.'

Max could have kissed him. Indigestion.

He might have told them the truth as soon as he returned home, but firstly, they wouldn't allow him to get a word in edgeways, and then when he did have the opportunity, he had already decided that there were ways in which the situation could be turned to his advantage. It didn't pay to rush straight into things without careful consideration.

Coming into the house, he slumped into a chair, still flabbergasted by what the doctor had told him. 'Are you okay, Dad?' Shane asked after exchanging a concerned glance with Madge.

'I went to the doctor's.' He intended to tell them then what the doctor had said, but Shane interrupted him.

'You should have said. I would have gone with you.'

'Poor Max.' Madge was shaking her head sorrowfully. 'You must have been in great pain to go so suddenly without telling us.'

'Well?' Shane demanded impatiently. 'What did he say?'

'The truth, son,' Max said flatly. 'Nothing more nor less than that. That's what I wanted to hear.' Again, he was about to tell them what the verdict had been, but then Madge let out a sob.

'Oh, Max. You took it like the man you've always been.'

Max began to protest. 'Now, listen, Madge . . .'

She sat down next to him. She took his hand. There were tears in her eyes. 'No, Max, *you* listen.' She spoke brokenly; tears coursed down her cheeks. 'I want to tell you how sorry I am for not taking your heart problem seriously. There were times when I thought it was just indigestion, and that you were making a song and dance about it. Oh . . .' she sobbed loudly . . . 'I feel so awful now.'

Max shifted uncomfortably on his feet. 'You weren't to know.'

'I know how Auntie Madge feels,' Shane said. His eyes were glistening, too. 'I admit I thought you were

135

swinging the lead sometimes . . . and now this.' He looked thoroughly woeful. 'Gee, what can I say?'

Max wished he could get a word in, but now Madge was having another go. 'You're not to worry about a thing from now on, Max,' she assured him warmly. She patted his hand. 'You've got two strapping sons, and you know I would do anything to help you.'

It was then that Max gave up trying to get a word in. An idea was beginning to form. His heart, that organ over which everyone was currently showing such concern, was beginning to lift. He looked at Madge with her tear-stained cheeks. 'Do you really mean that, Madge?' he asked hopefully. 'You'd do anything to help me?'

'Anything,' she whispered.

Max had to be careful here; he knew he was getting into deep water. But greed was greed; it was getting the better of him. 'This house,' he said faintly. 'I always dreamed of owning it completely . . . in time to leave it to my kids. If you signed it over to me, I'd have that peace of mind for whatever time I've got left.'

There – the lie was told. Madge choked back another sob.

Having decided that once he was on a good thing he should stick to it, while at the same time feeling more than a little guilty, Max justified it by telling himself that to all intents and purposes, he could slowly recover from his illness without giving the game away. It happened all the time; people recovered from serious illnesses; there was nothing unusual about that.

Madge was preparing lunch when Jim Robinson came in from next door. 'Come in, Jim,' she greeted him. 'You're just in time to talk some sense into this brother of mine.'

They had been arguing over what he should eat; Madge was taking her responsibilities very seriously.

'What's the problem?' asked Jim.

'He likes all the wrong food.'

'Give the man what he wants,' Jim said with a sympathetic glance at Max who was conserving his energy on the living room couch. 'He's going to complain until you do.'

'Yes,' Madge conceded. 'I tend to forget that you know him as well as I do.' She turned to her brother. 'All right, Max, what would you really like for lunch?'

Max gave it some thought. There was a number of possibilities. He chose one. 'I fancy a nice piece of fried tripe, with a few peas and home-made chips – nice and crispy.'

Madge grimaced. 'I give in,' she said, returning to the kitchen.

'The same old Max,' Jim said with a grin. 'You never admit defeat, do you?'

Max looked away in embarrassment. 'A man can't do that,' he muttered. 'Got to keep the old chin up.'

'And I admire you for it,' Jim said seriously as he reached into his pocket. 'I'd be really pleased if you'd accept this as a token of a long and solid friendship.' He held out a gold wristwatch.

Max forgot his embarrassment for the moment; it was a fine looking watch. He remembered it. 'The cross country race,' he said, taking the watch from Jim. 'When we were thirteen.'

'It's yours. You almost won it, anyway.'

Max strapped the watch around his wrist and stared at it admiringly. Yes, a very handsome watch. 'I couldn't take it, Jim.'

'Please,' Jim insisted. 'You've been a good mate to me over the years.'

Max was deeply moved. 'And you, too, Jim. All right. I'll wear it as a favour to you. I can watch my last days tick by on it.'

He made a great show of quiet suffering. He sighed a lot and played his Mantovani record. 'Isn't that a little depressing?' Madge asked.

Max sighed again. 'It's how I feel.'

She patted him on the shoulder and took the record off the turntable. 'It's no good upsetting yourself. You'll only make things worse.'

'Is that possible?'

Madge sat down opposite him. 'Max, you have every right to be miserable, but for Danny and Shane – for their sakes, you must keep your spirits up.'

'You're right, Madge.' Max's expression was one of gritty determination. 'They need me, and here I am, thinking only of myself.'

'If there's anything I can do,' Madge said gently. 'If there's any way I can lighten the load...'

Reaching across, Max gratefully clasped her hand in both of his. Yes, there was something... something that had been touched upon earlier. 'When I go,' he said with a sad smile, 'I want... it to be at home, not in a hospital. A man's got a right to die in his own home.'

'Of course he has.'

'Not that it's really *my* home,' he reminded her. 'I know that... the great Aussie tradition of owning your home, your own little corner of the world... and I never made it...'

He knew it was an excellent performance; he could see how it was affecting Madge, who said, much to his silent jubilation, 'Of course you will. I promise you. I'll speak to my solicitor and arrange to have the ownership transferred.'

'You're a good woman, Madge.' Releasing her hand, he slumped back against the pillows.

Everything was going along swimmingly. The family fussed over him. Shane brought him a bed tray and Danny a book on indoor gardening. Max enjoyed being pampered. Then, suddenly, everything changed. They stopped fussing over him.

Max realised something was wrong that morning when Danny and Shane refused to fix breakfast for him, after telling him that Madge had had to go out for some reason.

'But I'm a sick man,' Max said petulantly.

'Exactly,' Danny said with a shrug. 'You're not going to be around for much longer, so why should we tire ourselves out looking after you?'

Max had never heard anything so callous. Moments earlier, he had come into the kitchen, appreciatively sniffing the aroma of frying bacon. He had tucked the napkin under his chin with great expectation, and waited – and waited, while Shane wolfed up his own bacon and eggs and Danny hid himself behind the morning newspaper. Max was speechless.

Still hungry – starving, in fact – he wandered next door where his reception wasn't much better. Jim had just made himself a cup of coffee. He looked up coldly as Max walked into the kitchen through the back door. 'Good day,' Max greeted him affably. 'I just thought I'd put off going to work for a bit and see how my old mate is.' He eyed Jim's coffee. 'I could do with one of those myself. I didn't get any breakfast this morning.'

'If you want something you'll have to get it yourself,' Jim said unpleasantly. 'Some of us *do* have things to do.'

Max was well and truly puzzled. What *was* going on? Why had everyone so suddenly turned against him, a sick man, a dying man? 'What's happening?' he queried. 'Suddenly, everyone's giving me the cold shoulder.' He tried to make a joke of it. 'I mean, is it something not even my best friend can tell me?' Jim said nothing; he sat stonily at the table, sipping his coffee. 'Come on, Jim,' Max said with an uncertain laugh. 'One minute I'm the flavour of the month; and now...'

'I suppose we've all been somewhat over-sentimental,' Jim remarked. Max stared at him uncomprehendingly. 'And speaking of being over-sentimental,' Jim went on, 'I'd like my watch back, please.'

'But I thought you wanted me to have it.'

'I've been thinking about it,' Jim said brutally. 'It's not as if you'll be needing it, is it?'

Max was aghast. 'That's a bit cold-blooded, isn't it? They're not exactly hammering the lid on yet, are they?'

'I'll be around for it this afternoon,' Jim told him.

It was all very mystifying. Later that day, when he overheard a conversation between Madge and Helen Daniels, it became downright horrifying.

Clive had just given him a message that Helen wanted to see him about something. Max's glum mood lifted a little. Helen Daniels – now *there* was someone who would give him a sympathetic hearing. Helen was a warm and wonderful woman; she was a humanitarian. His heart full of hope, he went across to the Robinson house. The front door was open. He knocked, but there was no reply. Tentatively, he walked into the house. He could hear Helen's voice in the kitchen.

'It's not an easy decision you have to make, Madge,' she was saying. 'I wouldn't want to be in your shoes.'

So Madge was there as well. Max stood near the kitchen doorway and listened. He was suddenly apprehensive; he sensed they were talking about him. 'No, and I've got the boys' future to think about as well,' Madge said dolefully. 'They can't be expected to spend their lives looking after a decrepit old man.'

Decrepit? Max stood rigidly by the door. *Decrepit*? Him? It *was* him they were talking about, wasn't it? 'So have you found a place for him yet?' Helen asked.

'Yes, I had a look at it this morning. Twilight Hours, it's called – and I must say it looks as though it's a very well run sort of establishment. No nonsense, if you know what I mean. Strict rules. It will be just what he needs.'

'Is it very far away?'

'Far enough,' Madge said. 'There's no public transport, so he won't be able to just wander off, which is good.' Max felt weak. The colour had drained from his face. They *were* talking about him. 'Mind you,' Madge went on, 'I can't see that he would have the opportunity, anyway. The security's very good. Bars on the windows, that sort of thing, so the ... patients ... can't do any damage to themselves. All precautions taken. Yes, it will be more than suitable,' she added. 'The food's plain, of course, but nutritious. There's porridge for breakfast. Plenty of cabbage and boiled fish. Tuna casserole with ice cream to follow on Sundays as a special treat.'

'It must have been hard to find such a place for him,' Helen remarked. 'Some of them are booked out for years ahead.'

'It was, but this place had a couple of vacancies, owing to ... well, let's say departures to a better world.'

Listening to them in mounting horror, Max's worst fears were confirmed. They were out to get him. He was a marked man. 'When will you be taking him?' Helen asked.

'This weekend. He's getting worse all the time, so I think we'd better get it over and done with.'

'Well, let me know if I can be of any help.'

'Thanks, Helen,' Madge said warmly. 'It's been a trying time for all of us. But the end's in sight now. Max will be much happier there. Oh, now look at the time,' she said more urgently. 'I'd better be getting back.'

Hurriedly, as he heard footsteps coming towards him from the kitchen, Max backtracked along the hall to the front door, reaching it just as Helen and Madge appeared. As far as they were concerned – he hoped – he had just entered the house and hadn't heard a thing. He hoped they wouldn't see through the false heartiness with which he greeted them.

'Sorry to barge in, Helen. Clive gave me your message.'

'Oh yes, of course. Jim's lawnmower. Could we have it back, please?'

It was a deflating thing for Max to hear – and was that a fleeting smirk on the face of his sister who had just booked him into a nursing home? 'Yeah . . . right.'

'Poor Max,' Madge said with ineffable kindness as she studied his face. 'You've been looking so listless lately.' She took his arm and led him back to the door. 'Now don't you worry about a thing. We're all gong to take very good care of you.'

That conversation wasn't the only one Max was to inadvertently overhear that day. The one he overheard between Madge and the boys that afternoon was even worse. He had just come in through the back door with a bunch of flowers he had picked for Madge from the garden when he heard Danny in the living room, saying rather querulously, 'But, Auntie Madge, do you think that's fair?'

'Of course it is, Danny,' Madge replied. 'Max won't even know I haven't transferred the house over to him. It would be just a complete waste of time and money.'

Max stood rooted to the spot. Once again he was the topic of conversation. 'But what will you tell him?'

'Nothing. I'll put him off somehow. Anyway, he won't be around long enough to find out.'

A moment earlier, Max had been feeling quite robust; now he was feeling sick again. 'But what if he . . . you know . . . doesn't . . . ?'

'Yeah,' Shane said. 'What if the doctor's wrong about his heart?'

'Be patient, boys,' Madge advised them. 'You have my word. Your father *won't* be around much longer. If he doesn't go quietly – well, we'll just have to resort to Plan B.'

Plan B? Max clutched his bunch of flowers, some of which were already wilting. Nursing homes? Murder? Is that what they were really contemplating? Somehow, he had the feeling that things had gotten out of hand. In a daze, he wandered across to the living room where there was now silence, and where the sight that greeted him was one of pure nonchalance. They didn't even have the decency to look guilty.

'Max, you shouldn't be wandering about,' Madge gently admonished him as she came forward.

'That's right, Dad,' Danny said brightly enough. 'Every step could be your last. So you'd better save them while you can.'

Taking his arm, Madge shepherded him across to an armchair. 'Now you sit down right here and make yourself comfortable. I've got a nice surprise for you.'

A surprise? Plan B? Rat posion in the soup? He sat motionless, considering the possibilities, as Shane and Danny followed Madge out into the kitchen.

A moment later they were back. Shane was carrying a glass with ice cubes in it. Taking it across to the sideboard, he filled the glass half full of whisky while Max stared at him incredulously. Then Madge came in with a cake – and such a cake, with masses of whipped cream and cherries and slices of orange . . . She placed it on the table beside his chair. 'I baked it myself. It used to be your favourite – remember?' She smiled at the cake she had baked, then gave a delicious shudder. 'I could put on half a stone just looking at it.'

Max stared at the cake, then at the unbelievably stiff drink Shane had brought across to him. Plan B? A bad heart. There was something quite wolfish in the way everyone was smiling at him. 'You know what they say,' Madge said lightly. 'Eat, drink and be merry, for tomorrow . . .'

Max leapt to his feet and ran out of the house. He heard laughter behind him. His own family – he couldn't believe it! A gang of murderers, cut-throats, assassins! He went to see Des Clarke, who had to be about the only friend he had left.

'You *are* my mate, aren't you?' he demanded when Des showed signs of hesitation. If Des was about to turn against him too . . .

'Right on, Max.' He didn't sound altogether certain about it, though, Max noted.

'Those other fair weather ratbags have stabbed me in the back,' Max cried indignantly. 'After all I've done for them. The way they were carrying on at my place tonight, you'd reckon they couldn't wait to have me six feet under.'

Des was looking ill at ease. 'Well, I'm sure that's not true,' he said hesitantly.

Max stared at him closely. 'Now it's funny you should say that.' He began to bear down on Des who backed nervously away from him. 'You see, they were so nice to me one minute, and then they suddenly changed.'

'People are funny.'

'Oh, they're flamin' hilarious,' Max snorted. 'Laughs all the way along the line. But I want to know why I'm suddenly getting the thin end of the wedge.'

'Well, Max . . . mate . . . I'm just as shocked as you are.'

Max placed his arm around Des's shoulder. 'I knew you would be. We trust each other, and I'd be very hurt if you were keeping anything back from me. I'd be very angry if I found out there was something important you weren't telling me . . .'

Des gulped. 'I had nothing to do with it, Max.'

'To do with what?' Max demanded. 'Why are my boys talking as though they're about to put strychnine in my cereal?'

'They know, Max,' Des said unhappily. 'They found

144

out from your doctor. It was Helen. She took little Lucy to see him about her sore throat. They got to talking. Your name came up. They know there's nothing wrong with your heart.'

Max gaped at him. They *knew*? Suddenly, Max really did feel ill as he thought of the reception that would be waiting for him at home ...

Seven

His son? This po-faced kid was his *son*? This kid that he disliked so much? This little horror? But Andrea had just informed him he was – and now, looking more closely at the brat with the glint of superiority in his knowing eye, Des Clarke saw what might have been certain resemblances. He was thoroughly dismayed.

'But are you sure he's mine?'

'There was no one else, Des.'

Des stared at the kid. The kid stared defiantly back at him. Des poured himself another glass of port; he needed it.

It had been a big enough shock, Andrea turning up on his doorstep like that, completely out of the blue, all the way from Perth. He should have slammed the door in her face right there and then. Even if they did have something going together once, he had known nothing about this precious little souvenir she had brought with her on her journey east.

'Why didn't you tell me you were having a baby?' Des was completely shaken by the news; his hand trembled as it held the glass.

'I'd already left Perth – remember? After your mother nagged you so much that you had to call it off with me.'

They had just finished dinner. 'But you could have told me about the baby.'

She had virtually invited herself to stay. Little Bradley had already shown his true colours when, Des, having asked him to turn the water off at the mains while he fixed a dripping tap, the kid had turned it back on again just as Des was about to replace the washer. 'Sorry,' Bradley had said without a trace of regret as Des had angrily mopped the kitchen floor.

'I didn't tell you because I knew you didn't love me. If you had, you would have defied your mother. So I raised Bradley on my own.'

'But I would have helped you with money.'

'Des, you were young and ambitious,' Andrea said earnestly. 'The last thing you needed was a wife you didn't love and a baby you didn't want.'

'That's it, Pops,' Bradley said, spooning up his second helping of ice cream.

'Don't call me Pops,' Des sharply rebuked him. 'If I'm your father, you can start treating me with a bit of respect.' He turned back to Andrea who had hardly changed at all in the years since he had last seen her. 'So you kept it a secret from me, on purpose.'

Andrea nodded. 'I was never going to tell you, but...' she seemed to be steeling herself for something... 'Des, I'm down on my luck at the moment. I've never asked you for anything, but for once I need you. Please let Bradley and me stay here for a while.'

'Of course.' Des was feeling rather guilty. 'You must stay.'

'So what are you going to tell the neighbours?' Bradley pushed his dish away.

Des was suddenly alarmed. The neighbours! 'Nothing. I mean, I must tell them *something* – but not the truth.' They wouldn't understand; Max Ramsay, for one, would be up in arms again.

'No sweat, Dad,' Bradley said easily as Des sombrely regarded his shining face and carefully brushed hair and wondered at the strange turns fate sometimes took. 'We'll tell some lies.'

'Bradley,' Andrea said sharply, 'if you want to stay here, you'd better not open your mouth. Des is a bank manager, and he can't have any sort of a scandal. And if *I'm* going to be living here I certainly don't want the neighbours thinking I have an illegitimate son.'

'What do you usually tell people?' Des asked her.

'I say I was married and divorced when Bradley was still a baby.'

'That's it then.' It was an easy enough solution. 'That's what we'll say then.' He looked again at his son. 'All clear, Bradley?'

Bradley stared guilelessly back at him. 'How much pocket money will you be giving me?'

'Bradley . . .' Andrea held up a warning finger, Bradley shrugged carelessly and slid down in his chair.

Drawing obscene pictures was bad enough, but letting down Max Ramsay's tyres was quite something else again. When a furious Max, catching up with him, clipped his ear, Bradley came howling back into the house. Andrea was perturbed. 'Bradley! What happened?'

The howling stopped abruptly. A sly look came into the boy's eyes. 'A man hit me. Out there.' He pointed. 'A man with curly hair.' Des knew he was referring to Max Ramsay.

'How dare he!' Andrea was livid.

'I saw the whole thing.' Lucy Robinson had come in with Bradley who had already found himself on the wrong side of the girl's grandmother by telling her that he thought her paintings were so much rubbish.

'He hit me on the head,' Bradley complained. 'I could have brain damage.'

Taking his arm, Andrea hustled him to the door. 'Right. Show me where he lives.'

Des jumped to his feet in consternation. 'Hold on,

Andrea. Max Ramsay is a neighbour.'

Andrea tossed her head. 'Nobody hits my son and gets away with it.'

'But I'm already on bad terms with him,' Des protested. 'I don't want to make things worse.'

'I'm sorry, Des. I'm Bradley's mother.' She looked down at Lucy. 'Now show me where this Mr Ramsay lives.'

Lucy was only too happy to do so. Des groaned. Why did it have to be Max Ramsay of all the people in the street?

The next thing that happened was that Jim Robinson came home that afternoon to find that many of his prize roses had been decapitated and were lying strewn across the path. He was furious. He was picking them up when he saw a boomerang lying on the grass near one of the rose bushes. Then, seeing a movement behind another bush, he pounced and dragged out a wildly protesting Bradley. He marched him into Des's house. Andrea flared at Jim as she had flared at Max Ramsay when Bradley denied his culpability. Bradley was her son, her flesh and blood – she knew he wouldn't do anything like that. It was quite an ugly scene.

'You'll have to say something, Des,' Andrea said when he arrived home tired from a rather difficult day at the bank. 'No one's giving Bradley a chance.'

Des groaned inwardly. He had tried to get through to the boy, to make him understand that one had to get on with one's neighbours. People had to live peacefully together; they had to be considerate of each other. But he had made no impression whatever.

'Who's not giving him a chance?'

'The whole street. They're picking on him all the time.'

He looked at her doubtfully. Surely she had to be exaggerating. 'Oh, come on . . .'

'Well, some of them, anyway,' she amended. 'Jim Robinson. His son, and that other one – the delinquent who works in the bank with you.'

'Danny?' Des was puzzled. 'There's nothing wrong with him. Or with Scott Robinson. They're a couple of decent kids.'

'They bullied Bradley off his bike.'

Des found this hard to believe. 'Are you sure?'

'I'm not in the habit of telling lies,' she said haughtily.

'I didn't say you were.'

'Then stop talking as if I am.'

'Okay, okay, I'm sorry.' Des made a placating gesture. 'What was the run-in with Jim about?'

'Something petty. It's hardly worth mentioning.' Des continued to look at her. 'The boy was playing in his garden. Jim totally over-reacted, accusing him of setting out to destroy it.'

'But he didn't.'

'Of course he didn't.'

'You know,' Des said cautiously, 'it *is* possible that Bradley brings all his troubles on himself.'

'Why do you say that?' There was a hardness in Andrea's eyes.

'Getting on people's nerves,' Des replied. 'He's always up to something. That rubber spider in the medicine chest wasn't at all funny.'

'You're Bradley's father, Des,' Andrea said tightly. 'Don't you think it's about time you started acting like it?'

'I thought I was.'

'There's more to being a father than putting a roof over a child's head. You're supposed to support him – *not* come up with excuses for adults who act like bullies.'

Des's conscience was pricked. Perhaps she was right; perhaps there was something more that needed to be done. He sighed; he wasn't looking forward to it. 'All right then, I'll go and have a word with Jim. Danny and Scott, too – if I can find them.'

'Good,' Andrea said with a small, satisfied smile.

Des found Jim grimly surveying what remained of his prize roses. 'That little brat wrecked at least a dozen of my roses,' Jim said accusingly. 'And if you think that's over-reacting – count them.'

Des could see that Jim was still angry. 'I'm sure he didn't mean it.'

'The first couple – I agree,' Jim said. 'But he didn't stop there. He kept throwing that stupid boomerang.'

'What boomerang?'

'The kid had a boomerang. He obviously kept throwing it at the roses, seeing how many of them he could decapitate.' He regarded Des sourly. 'Now, *you* might think that kind of behaviour is okay – but I don't.'

'I didn't say it was,' Des returned defensively. 'But there's a right and wrong way to handle it. You didn't have to belt the kid.' It was what Andrea had told him Jim had done.

'I didn't belt him,' Jim said in a controlled voice. 'Des, the kid's an out and out brat. He had to be taught a lesson.'

'And you think violence is the answer?' Des was also becoming angry.

'Violence?' Jim stared back at him disbelievingly. 'Come on, Des. Don't you think you're taking this a bit far?'

Des didn't think so at all. 'Not when Scott has also been getting in on the act.'

'What are you talking about?'

'Pushing Bradley off his bike.'

'He didn't push Bradley off anything.'

'Well, bullied him off. Same thing.'

'The kid was riding on the footpath,' Jim told him. 'Which he shouldn't have been doing in the first place –

151

playing kamikaze with anyone who got in his way. Scott told him off, and if I'd been there I would have done the same thing.'

'Like father, like son,' Des said nastily.

'If you mean that neither of us will put up with an obnoxious, undisciplined little monkey – yes.' Jim's expression softened just a fraction. 'Quite frankly, Des, you'd be doing the street a hell of a favour if you got rid of the Townsends – mother *and* son.'

That evening, Andrea took special pains over dinner. There were candles on the table and a bottle of red wine had been opened. Bradley had been despatched early to bed. Des wondered how she had managed it.

'Here's to us,' Andrea said, raising her glass. She looked very seductive in the candlelight. 'We've lost each other, and now we've found each other again.'

Des was wary; he didn't know what was happening. He had come home from work to find all these elaborate preparations had been made. When he had asked her if she had invited someone for dinner, she had replied, no, there were only the two of them.

She smiled at him through the soft glow from the candles. 'What's so wonderful about it is that we get along so well together. I think we probably needed that time apart to mature.'

There was some reason behind it – that was for sure. Des gave a nervous laugh. 'Well, I *am* a little older.'

'We both are, Des. But the time we've had apart from each other – it's given me a chance to think. I've come to learn the important things in life, like a family, and security. Bradley's too young to put it into words, of course, but I know they're important to him too.'

'Yes, I suppose they must be,' Des said. The kid did need some stability in his life.

'I think it's every child's right to have a family.' Andrea was leaning forward in her chair. 'Don't you?'

152

Des could hardly say no to that. 'Yes.'

Putting down her glass, Andrea reached for his hand. 'Then why don't we give it to him, Des? The family he needs?'

Des felt himself suddenly trapped. 'Ah ... how?'

Andrea's smile was gentle. 'By getting married.'

Thoroughly trapped. Des didn't know what to say. 'Of course, I don't expect you to say "yes" right now. I know it's sudden. It's come as a shock to you. After all, we're both mature enough to know that marriage isn't something to be taken lightly.'

Desperately, Des was trying to find a way out of this predicament in which he so suddenly found himself. 'It's a total commitment,' he muttered.

'A commitment to one's responsibilities.' She nodded slowly. 'And in our case, Bradley is our responsibility. Now is our chance to face up to that. He really does need a stable home.'

'I intend to give him one,' Des promised.

She was smiling at him again. 'Once you thought I was very attractive.'

'You still are.'

'Surely we could try to make a go of it.'

'I can't.'

'We can overcome everything if we put enough effort into it.'

'The thing is ... Andrea ...' he cast about for the right words ... 'I don't want a relationship with anybody.' He had been stung often enough before. Five times he had been on the verge of marriage; five times something had gone wrong at the last minute.

'Not even with your own son?'

His own son. 'I'll father him as best I can.' And try to keep him out of trouble, although God knew, that wouldn't be easy. Yes, he definitely had a responsibility there. 'But with you – no.' He shook his head, then

153

added, more as a sop to her pride than anything else, 'Not yet, anyway.'

He wondered why she was smiling at him with such supreme confidence.

STAR BOOKS BESTSELLERS

0352319488	**The Equalizer**	**£1.95***
0352319496	**The Equalizer 2**	**£1.95***
0352320354	IAN DON **Tough Guys**	**£1.95***
0352316942	STEPHEN GRAVE **Miami Vice 1: The Florida Burn**	**£1.95***
0352316985	**Miami Vice 2: The Vengeance Game**	**£1.95***
0352317590	**Miami Vice 3: The Razor's Edge**	**£1.95***
0352317671	**Miami Vice 4: China White**	**£1.95***
0352320222	**Miami Vice 5: Probing by Fire**	**£1.95***
0352320451	**Miami Vice 6: Helhole**	**£1.95***
0352316454	SHAUN HUTSON **Terminator**	**£2.50**

STAR Books are obtainable from many booksellers and newsagents. If you have any difficulty tick the titles you want and fill in the form below.

Name _____

Address _____

_____

Send to: Star Books Cash Sales, P.O. Box 11, Falmouth, Cornwall, TR10 9EN.

Please send a cheque or postal order to the value of the cover price plus:
UK: 55p for the first book, 22p for the second book and 14p for each additional book ordered to the maximum charge of £1.75.

BFPO and EIRE: 55p for the first book, 22p for the second book, 14p per copy for the next 7 books, thereafter 8p per book.

OVERSEAS: £1.00 for the first book and 25p per copy for each additional book.

While every effort is made to keep prices low, it is sometimes necessary to increase prices at short notice. Star Books reserve the right to show new retail prices on covers which may differ from those advertised in the text or elsewhere.

*NOT FOR SALE IN CANADA

STAR BOOKS BESTSELLERS

		ELAINE ROCHE	
		Chateauvallon 1: The Berg	
△	0352320109	**Family Fortune**	£2.50
△	0352320117	**Chateauvallon: New Money**	£2.50
		CARL RUHEN	
△	0352317396	**Sons and Daughters 1**	£2.25
△	035231740X	**Sons and Daughters 2**	£1.95
△	0352319739	**Sons and Daughters 3**	£2.25
△	0352319879	**Sons and Daughters 4**	£2.25
△	0352320656	**Sons and Daughters 5**	£2.25
△	0352321083	**Neighbours**	£2.25*

STAR Books are obtainable from many booksellers and newsagents. If you have any difficulty tick the titles you want and fill in the form below.

Name _____

Address _____

_____

Send to: Star Books Cash Sales, P.O. Box 11, Falmouth, Cornwall, TR10 9EN.

Please send a cheque or postal order to the value of the cover price plus:
 UK: 55p for the first book, 22p for the second book and 14p for each additional book ordered to the maximum charge of £1.75.
BFPO and EIRE: 55p for the first book, 22p for the second book, 14p per copy for the next 7 books, thereafter 8p per book.
OVERSEAS: £1.00 for the first book and 25p per copy for each additional book.

While every effort is made to keep prices low, it is sometimes necessary to increase prices at short notice. Star Books reserve the right to show new retail prices on covers which may differ from those advertised in the text or elsewhere.

*NOT FOR SALE IN CANADA